THE KING-BORN

The life of Olaf the Viking,
King of the Danes and
King of England

By

Ian Fraser

V7

Published by sifipublishing 2012

info@sifipublishing.co.uk

www.sifipublishing.co.uk

first published in 1989.

ISBN: 978-0-9572640-1-4

The 13th century seal of the town of Grimsby in Lincolnshire. 'Grimsby' means 'Grim's village'; and the Grimsby seal shows Grim like a giant guarding Havelock and Goldenburg. (Note: Havelock is an English form of the Scandinavian name Olaf.) Grim is holding a sword and a shield and has what appears to be a helmet between his feet; Olaf is holding an axe and a helmet; and Goldenburg is holding a distaff. There are small crowns above the heads of Olaf and Goldenburg, to show their royal destiny.

CONTENTS

Introduction

INTRODUCTION

Human beings in a simple state of civilisation have usually believed that their kings were gods. They believed this in Egypt, Greece and other Middle Eastern countries long before Christ; and they believed it until quite recently in some parts of Asia. There are few records of Northern Europe in the ancient times when Northern Europeans fully believed that kings were gods; but in England at least they half believed it throughout the Middle Ages. Medieval Englishmen did not believe that their kings were actually gods; for they believed in the One Christian God. But they did believe that kings were unlike other people. For instance, they thought that kings possessed special divine birthmarks, divine powers of healing and a divine right to do whatever they wanted. They believed that a man born to be a king would overcome all difficulties; and they believed that anyone who hurt or wronged him would be pitilessly crushed by the avenging gods.

The story in this book was often told by English minstrels in the period 1100-1400A.D.; but it describes England and Denmark before England was conquered by the Normans; and it may be an account of the Danish conquest of England in 1013. The names of the people are not historical; but their thoughts and actions are probably true to life at that faraway time.

We of the 20th century find it difficult to believe many things in this story; but there is nothing in it which was incredible to a medieval Englishman; for both his thoughts and his feelings were at least as different from ours as were his clothes and language.

THE
KING-BORN

CHAPTER I

THE KING'S WILL

Although it was nearly a thousand years after Christ, the Danes were still more pagan than Christian; and their fierce chiefs had been held together under the leadership of a single king for only a few years.

The Danish King's camp was beside Jelling Creek in eastern Denmark. Sweeping wide around the camp there was a circular ditch and a massive wall of earth and logs; and within this wall there were many buildings. But there was not a stone nor a brick nor a tile in the whole huge camp. The walls of the buildings were made of tarred boards or of wickerwork smeared with clay; and their roofs were made of golden-grey reed thatch or of mottled skins. Among the buildings, log-roads and wooden boardwalks seemed to float on a sea of shiny black mud; for the camp itself was almost as wet as Jelling Creek outside.

In the fenced boatyards beside the creek many ships and boats were drawn up above the high-water mark. Most of them were too small even for a mast; but there were nearly a hundred seventy foot long warships called 'longships'; and there were also two a hundred and forty foot long warships called "dragonships." Long, wide and shallow, the ships were blacker than the mud around them; for they were tarred; and their high gilded prows and sternposts had been stowed out of harm's way. But here and there a painted gunnel or a chequered sail hung up to dry, coloured the gloom.

In the very middle of the vast, dismal camp stood the King's high hall. It was a simple building, like a long, narrow barn; but its roof was bright with new golden thatch; and its boarded walls and gables were gaily painted. The King's Hall looked gay among the other buildings; but it was closely guarded by a ring of twelve tarred barrack-huts, shaped like large boats turned upside down. In those black barracks lived the five hundred men who crewed the King's ships; for they had sworn to guard him in return for food in his hall. The King and his guards were protected by an inner stockade and ditch; for in those days a king was not safe, even when surrounded by his sworn hearthmen and in his own camp.

On that rainy October day the King's camp was unusually crowded; for ten thousand Danish warriors had come back with him after a victorious battle against the Swedes. But in spite of the crowds and the glorious victory the camp was hushed and ill at ease. On the wooden boardwalks many groups of men stood with their backs turned to the driving drizzle. They whispered hoarsely and gripped their weapons with restless hands. Each chieftain had posted look-outs to watch the other chiefs; and every man was ready at a word either to fight or to sail away.

In all that great camp only warriors were visible; for the women and children and slaves were skulking behind double-barred doors. In the women's hall the children had been herded into the crimson darkness near the smoky fire; and the slave-women were telling them stories, to hush their whimpering. But the ladies peered out through cracks in the wooden walls and doors, timidly watching the scowling, snarling men.

The whole camp was tense with fear of doom and death. For only King Magnus could control the quarrelsome Danish earls and his own wild hearthmen; and the great king was dying.

The King's private bower was at the inner end of the high hall in the middle of the camp. There he lay on a rug of beaver skins, which was spread on a hard mattress between four stubby bedposts. Those bedposts were carved into fierce faces and painted red, to frighten evil spirits; but the faces of the three little children who stood beside the bed were white with strain and wide-eyed with fear. Olaf and his two sisters watched the King with agonised attention.

Olaf could see that the man on the bed had his father's big body and long golden hair; and the man had also his father's bushy beard and wide moustaches pointed like an ox's horns. Nevertheless, he seemed almost a stranger. Olaf was only five; and he still lived with his sisters in the women's hall; for in those days boys did not eat and sleep with the warriors, until they were seven. He had met his father only rarely, when his father had sent for him in order to play with him. The father whom he knew was red faced and noisy with life and laughter; and he had never seen his father still and silent even in sleep.

Olaf had often seen men and animals who were sick and dying; and he knew that the man on the bed was near death. The face on the wooden pillow was as pale as a tallow candle; and the muscular arms lay on the beaver skins as limply as old ropes. Only the massive legs stirred restlessly beneath the furs which covered them; and the deep chest, thickly wrapped in bloody bandages, heaved desperately for breath.

Slowly Olaf understood that his kindly playmate was buried inside the pale carcass on the bed. The sharp pain of losing his father stabbed at his belly through the numbness of his fear; and he felt sick with loneliness. But for comfort he could hold hands only with his sisters; for his mother had died when he was born; and he was afraid of his uncle, Earl Thorard, who stood behind him with his heavy hands on Olaf's shoulders.

Suddenly the King tossed feverishly and heaved himself up onto one elbow. He was a mighty ruin of a man; and his straw-coloured beard and white skin were streaked and spattered with blood. For a long while he fought for air; and his blue eyes bulged fiercely at his shorter, black-haired brother. Then, with his breath whistling in his throat, he began to speak.

"Brother Thorard, when I am dead, you must guard my children as if they were your own. You must hold together the Kingdom of the Danes, until Olaf is old enough to do so himself; and you must look after my daughters."

"Never fear, Lord. I will provide for your children."
Earl Thorard said and humbly bent the knee.

The King beckoned the other Danish earls, who stood around the walls, to come nearer to his bed; and he called the Christian priest, who was his secretary and the only man in the camp who could write. The King's eyes blazed in his white face; the bandages around his wounded chest gleamed wet with fresh, bright blood; and his breath rasped in and out like a saw. But whenever he could find strength, words spouted from his mouth in tumbling torrents of command.

"Now hear my will, you Great Men of the Danes." The voice grated like a steel file on the edge of a sword. "And let my words be written down; for you must remember them, when I am gone to hunt with my fathers, the gods.

Firstly, Olaf, my son, shall follow me; and he shall be the King of the Danes, when he is a man. Until that time, let it be known by all the Danes that the boy is holy. HOLY!" he shouted and with the effort coughed blood onto his beard "For the blood of kings runs in Olaf's veins; and the fiery breath of the Danish gods burns in his breast. If any man lifts his hand to harm Olaf, that man shall lose both his life and all his belongings.

Secondly, Thorard, my younger brother, shall be the Guardian of the Kingdom, while Olaf is a boy. But my son Olaf shall be King, as soon as he can put the weight further than Thorard and can throw him at wrestling.

Thirdly, I, Magnus, must leave you very soon. When I no longer breathe, put me out to sea in my pleasure-ship." After a while he added in a hoarse whisper, "For I must sail away, to join my fathers, the gods."

Olaf was numb with fear and loneliness; but his eyes and ears were wide open; and he never forgot what he heard and saw that day.

As the King struggled to hold off death for a little while, he panted for breath; and he glared fiercely at his captains, as though daring them to gainsay his will. Then he turned to the shaven-headed priest, saying sharply: "Wax!"

While the priest heated a lump of black wax, the King ruled his men with his fierce eyes; but his right hand was groping about on the beaver skins which covered him. The searching hand became frantic; and his fierce eyes became shifty with doubt and dread; for, since he was grown-up, King Magnus had never once been without his sword, even at night. A scornful smile stirred the black beard around Earl

7

Thorard's lips; but suddenly a short, thickset man, whose leathery face was deeply scarred, ran to the King's side. The stocky warrior drew the King's sword from its wolfskin scabbard, as it hung on a bedpost; and, kneeling humbly, he put the sword's hilt into the King's right hand. "Ah, good Ubbe! My little sword-brother!" The grateful King said; and he glared triumphantly at Thorard.

The priest dropped a blob of melted wax onto the parchment below his writing; and Earl Ubbe helped the king to press the moulded pommel of his sword into the soft wax. The King stared at the raven's head printed on the wax. "The King-mark!" he grunted; and a half-smile twisted the corners of his mouth. Then he said to the priest: "Write 'Magnus' beside the raven."

With a laugh King Magnus clawed at the bandages around his chest and uncovered a deep gash dark with blood. He made the priest dip his quillpen into the heart's blood welling from the wound. The priest had lived among the fierce Danes for fully five years; but he was a Rhinelander born and bred; and, although he obeyed and wrote "Magnus" in blood beside the King's seal, he shuddered with disgust.

"Now you as first witness, Thorard!" the King shouted, glaring at his brother. But Thorard had seen the King's dismay when he found himself weak and weaponless; and his lifelong fear of his huge brother had gone out like the tide. So he grinned scornfully and scratched his nose with his thumb.

However, Thorard did not have time to refuse his brother's command. With a catlike spring, Ubbe was beside him and holding a sharp knife to his back. "Let the others bear witness first!" Thorard mumbled; for he hoped that the King might die, before he himself had to witness the will. But Ubbe pushed him within reach of the King's drawn sword.

"Not so!" the King growled fiercely. "You first, Thorard!"

The King's eyes were narrowed and keen; his sword-arm was bent, ready to strike; and the flickering light of the candles glinted on the filed edge of his sword. Scowling Thorard licked his lips in fear and lowered his eyes to the parchment. Reluctantly he pressed his sword-seal into the black wax below the King's seal; and he swore both on the White Christ's cross and on Odin's ring to do the King's will. Then at last the King let him go; and he slunk away into a dark corner and chewed his beard in anger.

One by one the chiefs swore the double oath and sealed the King's deathbed law. Then at last King

Magnus' fierce eyes grew dull; he gasped for breath and fell back wearily onto his pillow. With an effort he found Olaf's hand and held it tightly on the bed beside him. But soon Olaf felt his father's grip loosen; and he saw that his father's chest no longer rose and fell with his breathing. Then he was led away to the women's hall, half-stunned by the horror and wonder of what he had seen.

That night, when darkness had fallen, Olaf was awoken; and he was carried aboard his uncle's dragon-ship. In the large ship thirty pairs of warriors sat on the thwarts, ready at their oars; One hundred warriors stood on the foredeck and along the central gangway; and twenty chiefs stood on the quarterdeck at the stern. Olaf was put down on the quarterdeck between Thorard and the steersman; and the Black Earl gave the order to cast off.

Olaf could not see much through the legs of the chiefs around him; but he saw Earl Ubbe standing watchfully, with his legs straddled and his back to the tall, gilded sternpost. Ubbe held his right hand near his sword-hilt; and he kept a wary eye on Thorard; for he knew that Thorard would want revenge for being humbled at King Magnus' deathbed. But Black Thorard was smiling and cheerful; for now he was the headman of the Danes; and he need no longer fear his bigger, elder brother.

While Thorard's men rowed the dragon-ship down the creek to the open sea, Olaf looked back towards the camp; and he saw that the dragon-ship was towing his father's "karfi" or pleasure-ship. thirty flaming torches were fastened to the karfi's sides; and the sixty painted shields on her gunnel and the gilded raven's head on her tall prow were bright with colour. But within the karfi it was dark; and nothing moved.

When the two ships had reached the open sea, Thorard ordered his men to stop rowing; and the smaller karfi was brought alongside. Then Thorard picked Olaf up in his arms and ran down a gangplank into the karfi.

Some of Thorard's men jumped down into the karfi, to unfurl and set the sail, which was gaily chequered red and yellow; but in the ship's dark belly abaft the massive mast, King Magnus lay on a bed of pine logs painted black with pitch. It looked to Olaf as though his father had gone to sleep in his battle-shirt of iron mail. But the King's gilded helmet, his axe, his sword and his long spear lay near his hands on the bed; and beside the bed lay his best horse and favourite hounds, all with their throats slit, all dead.

Thorard and the twenty chiefs gathered silently around the King's bed. Thorard put Olaf down on the deck near the King's head; and in his hands he placed one of the lighted torches from the gunnel. Thorard himself and each of the chiefs also took a torch; and they raised them high above their iron helmets. Humbly they bent the knee and bowed their heads. Then they shouted: "Greetings, Lord Magnus! A thousand greetings!"

Olaf watched the King, hoping to see him sit up and answer the greeting of his men; but the King was fast asleep and never stirred. Suddenly Olaf felt a tap on the shoulder.

"Step forward, my child," the Black Earl told him, "and lay your torch against the logs below your father's head."

Everyone was so solemn that Olaf did not dare to question his uncle. He laid the flaming torch at the foot of the log-bed below his father's shining golden hair. But, when he looked at his father's still, pale face, he burst into tears; and he hammered his fists on the grey iron rings covering the King's chest.

"Lord Father! Lord Father!" Olaf cried, as he tried to awaken the dead. But Thorard scooped him up and pressed him against his greasy mail shirt; and the knobbly rings digging into Olaf's cheek made him forget his father. Olaf put forth all his childish strength, to free himself from the pain. But Thorard held him tight and muffled his cries in his musty fur cloak.

Thorard laid his torch against his brother's bed; and the other chiefs stepped forward one by one, to light the funeral pyre. But suddenly, when Ubbe passed him, Thorard stumbled and dropped Olaf sprawling under Ubbe's feet. Olaf, lying on the deck, saw a flash of steel in Thorard's hand. But the watchful Ubbe held his torch on guard and snatched his knife from his garters.

For a moment the two earls crouched over Olaf, face to scowling face. Then with one accord they turned aside and put their knives away, as though nothing unusual had happened. Ubbe laid his torch against the logs; and, being a good Christian, he crossed himself and said a prayer. Finally he touched his dead lord's hand in fond farewell and went back to his place. But he took care not to go near the grinning Thorard.

The tar in the funeral bed began to hiss and to spurt blue flames; and the pine logs at the bottom of the pile began to crackle and spit. Soon King Magnus lay on a narrow raft of darkness above a golden sea of fire. As the chiefs standing round the bed watched their King, their faces ran with sweat; but Olaf cowered away from the fierce heat and crept into the shadows in the stern.

The flames rose higher; and the heat grew fiercer, until the chieftains' eyes watered with pain. but, although their faces were scorched red, they did not flinch. Suddenly Thorard turned on his heel and strode up the gangplank, back into his own ship; and the chiefs and seamen gladly followed him. The moorings were cut; Thorard's ship pulled away from the dangerous flames and sparks; and the blazing karfi lapped and lolloped in the swell, with no one to sail her except the dead King.

"Ho! Where is the boy?" cried Ubbe.

"Where is Olaf Magnusson?" asked the chiefs.

Black Thorard looked around his ship. "Olaf, where are you?" he called.

"There he is, in the King's ship," Ubbe shouted, pointing across the water to the small yellow head shining in the firelight. "Go alongside; and take him off at once," Ubbe told the steersman.

Thorard had hoped that Olaf would be forgotten until it was too late to save him; but even in his own ship he did not dare to belay Ubbe's order.

"Yes! Fetch him back," he said and forced a laugh. "What a silly little knave to get left behind at a funeral!"

With a few strokes of her sixty oars, the big dragon-ship again drew alongside the blazing karfi; and a seaman jumped down into the smaller ship. The seaman took Olaf on his shoulders and swarmed up a leather line back into his own ship. Thorard stepped forward to take Olaf; and he poked him in the ribs, saying with a mocking grin: "Your father did not mean that you should follow him like THAT, foolish boy."

Faithful Ubbe looked grim; and the other chiefs laughed half-heartedly; for they all distrusted the sly Earl Thorard.

A gentle breeze filled the karfi's sail; the flames mounted about the golden King; and the funeral-ship rapidly bore away into the darkness. While Thorard's ship followed slowly with paddling oars, the priests of Odin whirred iron rattles, to frighten away evil spirits; and the Christian priest prayed loudly in Latin, asking the White Christ to take King Magnus' soul. But the simple warriors were silent with awe, as the King's ship caught fire from stem to stern.

Suddenly there sounded a gusty "Ahhh!" of wonder from all the men in Thorard's ship; and Olaf saw that the fire had swallowed the karfi's sail. Now flames were leaping from the karfi's mast towards the clouds, which were piled like snow-clad mountains in the sky. Thorard pointed towards the fiery giant dancing in the darkness.

"There goes your father, Olaf, leaping aloft to hunt with the gods," he said in admiration.

The chiefs and warriors raised their voices in a last loud farewell to their warrior-king; but Olaf stared silently, until the distant flames died down to a glow. Then, shaken by sobs, he buried his face against the musty fur of his uncle's cloak. He disliked his uncle; but he felt weak and very lonely; and there was no one else to give him comfort.

CHAPTER II

THE WICKED UNCLE

F or some months after the King's death Olaf and his sisters lived in the same way as before. They ate and slept in the women's hall of their father's camp; they played at battles and weddings and other games with the children of his warriors; and they helped the bakers and the brewers, the metalworkers and the sailmakers, the grooms and the kennelmen. But they missed the noisy stir of the crowds which surround a king.

Before their father died, the camp had been full of his warriors and craftsmen; and there had been much coming and going of chiefs and ambassadors, traders and minstrels. But King Magnus' men soon found other masters to feed and shelter them; and, now that Earl Thorard was the Danish leader, few people came to visit King Magnus' camp.

King Magnus' children gradually lost touch with their father's friends, who lived in other camps; and the warriors, servants and slaves of their father's household went elsewhere. When spring came around, King Magnus' great camp was almost empty. Only a few old women and a hundred of Thorard's men kept the children company. Then one day in April Thorard Blackbeard himself was rowed up the creek in his big ship; and he took away King Magnus' children.

"I am taking you to my own camp, so that my wife can look after you," Thorard told the children; but his wife treated them as though she hated them. They were imprisoned in a damp, dark, cowhide tent, which stank of the salted whale-meat which had been kept there. They were fed only scraps of the food which was left over from the meals in Thorard's hall; and they grew pale and thin with hunger and misery.

When the children of Thorard's household came to the tent, they came only to tease and to bully. But one evening the Black Earl himself strode into the tent; and Olaf and his sisters gathered round their uncle with their complaints.

"Give us more food, Uncle. We are not dead, you know," the eldest girl said.

"I will very soon put that right," Thorard said with a laugh. "Come and sit on my lap, my dear little nieces."

The two girls ran to Thorard's arms. He sat one on each knee and, grinning gaily, cut their throats. Olaf

gaped with sickening horror; and, in abject fear of
Thorard's knife, he clapped his hands to his own
throat. Olaf tried desperately to run away; but his legs
were jellied; and Thorard laughed.

"You have nothing to fear, King-born," he jeered.
"By your dead father's will, no man may harm you on
pain of death. Enjoy your good luck, boy; and eat all
the food which I send you. For, if you do not eat well,
you will not grow strong; and then you will never be
able to put the weight further than me; and you will
never be able to throw me at wrestling."

Thorard walked away, laughing until the tears ran
down his cheeks; but he soon came back, carrying a
big, round stone; and Olaf saw that it was the
"weight" which warriors hurled for sport.

"Now, my young King, watch me put the weight.
Then you can try to do it," Thorard said with a grin.

He hurled the heavy stone half a ship's length and
sent Olaf to fetch it. Olaf could only just lift the stone
from the ground by kneeling down and using both
hands.

"Hurry up, little King!" Thorard roared.

In his fright Olaf dropped the weight on his foot.
He screamed with pain; but Thorard laughed and
slapped his thighs with mirth.

"Give me the stone, King-born," the Earl said and took it in one hand. "Now, let me see how far YOU can throw it."

Thorard tossed the heavy stone to Olaf; and it knocked him flat. The boy lay on the ground, whimpering with fright and gasping for breath. But Thorard picked him up and thumped his back and stroked his hair, saying scornfully: "Father's little darling!"

When Olaf had recovered his breath, Thorard said: "Now let us find out whether you can throw me at the wrestling!"

Thorard told Olaf to attack him with a leghold. Then he made him try an armhold and afterwards a beardhold. But, whatever Olaf did, Thorard threw him down with a flick of his wrist or a kick of his leg. In the end he threw the little boy right over his head; and Olaf fell heavily and lay moaning in a crumpled heap.

"You will never be strong enough to put the weight or to wrestle with ME." Thorard jeered, as he prodded him with his toe. "You will never be 'King Olaf the Strong;' but I have clothes and a task for which you ARE fitted. Get up!" he roared.

Thorard stripped off Olaf's woollen clothes and gave him a peasant's rough shirt of tarred canvas and a spade. He made Olaf dig a hole in a corner of the tent; and he made him bury the bodies of his sisters and his own clothes.

Thorard looked at Olaf with satisfaction. "Now you are no longer Olaf King-born," he said. "You are simply a naked, low-born churl."

Thorard rubbed his hands and grinned happily. Then he barred the door and went away, laughing.

Olaf trembled with fear and wept with misery, until, at last, he cried himself to sleep. But in the night he was awoken by Thorard's voice; and Thorard was saying, "Here he is, Grim. The little foundling has neither father nor mother; and he is a half-starved, misshapen little wretch. Nobody wants him. So carry him home in your sack; take him out to sea before daybreak; and send him right to the bottom in deep water."

Olaf jumped up in a cold sweat of terror; for he saw coming towards him two huge figures behind a torch. He tried to run away; but Thorard sprang forward and quickly caught him. Then Thorard put a gag in Olaf's mouth and tied him up with strips of canvas.

"Your father said that you should follow him; and so you shall — out to sea," Thorard whispered into Olaf's ear; and he laughed, as he kicked him towards

Grim. "Take the little churl," he ordered Grim, "and, when you have done your simple task, you shall have a gold ring and a good sword for reward," he promised.

Roughly Grim pushed Olaf into his smelly fish-sack. Then he tied its mouth and threw it onto his shoulder. Thorard's harsh laughter grew faint in Olaf's ears; and he was carried, bump-bumping all the way, to Grim's hut by the sea.

By the time that Grim had reached his hut, Olaf was moaning loudly; for his limbs were cramped in the small sack; and they ached terribly. But Grim cuffed him. "Be quiet, little wretch," he hissed at Olaf. "You will wake my three sons."

Grim opened the door and threw the sack onto the ground. Olaf squealed with pain. Grim kicked him hard and told him to be quiet; but Olaf heard a woman ask sleepily:

"What have you got, Grim? A fat pigling?"

"Not so, wife! It is only a foundling, whom Earl Thorard has told me to drown. It seems that the boy has neither father nor mother; and Earl Thorard says that the little wretch is so misshapen and starved that nobody wants him."

"And what did Earl Thorard give you for doing that?" Grim's wife asked sharply.

"He promised to give me a gold ring and a good sword when the task is done."

Grim's wife thought that much too rich a reward for so small a task as killing a nobody; and she said doubtfully, "I hope that he is as good as his word, Grim; but I don't trust Thorard, even though he is an earl. He swore a double oath to his brother, the good King Magnus, that he would look after Magnus' children. But you never see or hear of the children nowadays; and some folk say that Thorard has killed them so that he himself can be King."

"Don't talk so loudly," Grim muttered fearfully. "You never know who might be listening." Then he whispered: "We shall find out tomorrow the true worth of Earl Thorard's word; for I mean to take this little wretch with me when I go fishing. Wake me early, wife. I want to be at sea before it is light. Drowning boys is a task best done in the dark."

Grim untied the sack and let Olaf stretch out on the earth floor; and his wife smothered the glowing red embers of the fire with ashes and turfs. Then they went to sleep on a pile of rushes. Olaf wept silently, half-choked by his gag; but at last he too went to sleep, lying on the cold, bare earth.

The first cock crowed, to warn the fishermen that day was near; and Grim's wife rolled sleepily out of bed, to blow up the fire. She reached for the flint, to light the fat-lamp; but, as she opened her eyes, she saw that the hut was already light. "Ho, Grim! Wake up!" she cried, shaking him. "It is already day."

Grim threw off the rushes and looked out of the door. But he turned back angrily. "Wife, are you trying to make a fool of me?" he asked threateningly. "Out there it is still pitch-black."

Grim's wife put her hands to her mouth in fear. But it was not Grim of whom she was afraid. "It is dark outside; but it is light in here." she muttered in disbelief. "And yet I have neither lit the lamp nor opened up the fire." Then she gripped her husband's arm and pointed urgently. "Look! The light is coming from that foundling."

"You are right, wife." Grim agreed; but he shook his head in bewilderment. "The boy's face is bright; and the light in the hut comes from his mouth, behind the gag."

Grim bent over the sleeping boy and untied the gag. At once a beam of light shone from Olaf's mouth, like a sunbeam suddenly piercing the darkness of the hut. Grim's wife smothered a shriek with a hand over her mouth. Then she seized Grim's arm and whispered in his ear: "Oh, Grim! This is not a low-born foundling. My own mother was nurse to

King Magnus, when he was a boy; and she told me that at night a beam of light used to shine from the King-born's mouth. This boy is King-born too. He must be Magnus' son."

Grim scratched himself, while his slow mind moved. Then he shook Olaf awake. "Ho there, boy!" he said. "Tell me truly who you are and who was your father."

Olaf blinked and looked around in fright; but, seeing neither anger nor hatred in the faces bending over him, he answered proudly: "I am Olaf, the only son of King Magnus and nephew to Earl Thorard."

Grim's wife whispered to her husband: "My mother told me that King Magnus had a King-mark on his shoulder. Like a raven's head she said it was. Let us see if this boy has the King-mark too."

The fisherman and his wife looked on Olaf's shoulder; and they saw the King-mark, like a small drawing of the raven's head prow of King Magnus' ship or the seal of his sword. Hastily they untied Olaf and warmed his cold legs by the fire. They gave him salt fish to eat and a bowl of milk to drink. When Olaf had eaten, Grim knelt before him and said humbly: "King-born, forgive us for treating you roughly. We did not know you. Tell us how you came to be in my sack."

Olaf told Grim and his wife all about Thorard's wickedness. He told them about the killing of his two sisters; he told them about the brutal wrestling lesson; and he told them of Thorard's joke about sending Olaf to follow his father to the bottom of the sea. Olaf's memories frightened him; but Grim's wife held his head against her breast and gave him comfort.

Then Grim filled his sack with a log of wood and some stones; and he took it with him, when he went fishing. After he had 'drowned' the weighted sack, he gave his wife a fish for the King-born's dinner; and he went off to Thorard's camp, to get his reward.

When Grim came back, he slammed the door and angrily threw down his cloak.

"You were right to distrust Earl Thorard, wife," he grumbled. "He gave me his gold ring; but he put it on my cheek with his fist behind it; and he gave me his sword across my back. See here!" Grim showed her a dark bruise on his cheek and a long red weal on his shoulder blades. "I told the Earl that I had drowned the poor boy as he had ordered. But Thorard asked me whether I had seen anything unusual. 'Unusual?' I said. 'I do not USUALLY drown boys, I can tell you; and I did it this time, only because you promised to pay me well.'

26

'Yes, yes, yes!' the Earl said. 'But did the boy say or do anything?'

'No, Lord!' I said. 'He could neither speak nor move, because he was gagged and tied up by you. But, when I put the stones into the sack with him, I did see a sort of light coming from his mouth.'

'Ah!' the black-hearted Earl said with an evil grin: Do you know what that meant, fisherman?'

'No, Lord!' I said. 'I have never before seen anything like it.'

'Then I will tell you, Grim,' the Earl said, still grinning like a dog. 'That light comes from the breath of the gods; and the gods' breath burns only in the breasts of those who are Kings or born to be Kings. You have just drowned the young Lord Olaf, King Magnus' son and heir. Before King Magnus died, he made a mighty law, which was witnessed by all the great men of the Danes; and they undertook that if any man lifts his hand against Olaf, that man shall lose his life; and his wife and children shall be made slaves. Do you hear that, Grim? If any man lifts his hand against Olaf, that man shall lose his life; and his wife and children shall be made slaves,' Then he growled at me like a wolf," Grim said. "'Leave Denmark before tomorrow night,' he threatened; 'or else I shall tell the Great Men that you have killed the little King-born because you hate me. And do you know what they will do, Grim? They will skin you alive; and your wife and children they will sell as slaves.' "

Grim licked his lips in fear, as he repeated Thorard's terrible threat. But then his eyes flashed angrily. "When I asked the Earl for the rewards which he had promised me, he struck me, as you see; and I ran home in a rage."

"What an evil man Earl Thorard is! No! He is not a man. He is a devil," Grim's wife cried. "Do you think that he will tell the Great Men that you killed their King?" she asked fearfully.

"Yes, wife! I do indeed." Grim answered; but he added stoutly: "Tonight I shall work to make the boat ready; and you must sell all our belongings, to buy food and oak casks for a fortnight's journey. Tomorrow we shall set sail over the sea for England; for I have heard that England is a rich land and that her seas are full of fish."

CHAPTER III

THE VOYAGE TO ENGLAND

Grim's wife hid Olaf in the warmth of her bed and went off to sell the family's belongings. The fisherman and his three sons pulled Grim's boat up from the sea on rollers and turned it bottom-up beside the hut.: "I have dreamed a dream, my sons." Olaf heard Grim say "Mighty Magnus has told me to sail to the River Humber in England, to find better fishing. Your mother is selling our hut and our beehives, our sheep and our fowls; and you must sell your half-built boat, to buy food and drink."

Whilst the boys went to do as their father had ordered, Grim readied his sturdy old boat, for the long voyage across the open sea. He felt that the gods were helping him; for his body seemed stronger than before; and the daylight seemed to last longer than usual; and the moon seemed to shine more brightly than he had ever seen it. He was happy, because he was going to be a sea-faring Viking again. While he worked, he sang an old boatman's song.

29

Olaf thought that Grim was singing in order to tell him how he was making the boat ready for sea; for that was what the song was about. First Grim scraped clean the underwater timbers; then he caulked the seams with strips of cloth and resin glue; and he covered everything with a thick coat of tar. Later he cut a new foot on the mast; and he mended the square sail of criss-crossed strips of black and yellow cloth. Last of all he renewed the walrus-hide ropes; for the head of the sail was lashed to the pinewood spar with leather thongs; and the sheets for controlling the belly of the sail and the tackle for raising the spar were also made of leather.

Sometimes, without changing the tune of the old boatman's song, Grim sang his own words. He promised to carry the little raven to safety far from his foes; he said that one day he and his sons would bring the raven home again; and he undertook to kill all the raven's foes and to make their wives and children slaves. Olaf, wrapped warmly in the fisherman's bed, knew that Grim's song was about him; and he hugged himself with delight.

Grim's three sons joined him in working on the boat; and by the next afternoon she was ready for sea. At the evening high tide they launched her. They packed their clothes into a tarred sea chest and their food and drink into wooden casks. In oily hides they wrapped charcoal and a tinderbox; and they put on board clay pots for cooking and a long-legged iron pot to hold the fire itself. Lastly, after a hot meal, they wrapped the King-born in a warm sealskin; and they carried him with their fishing-nets and lines to the boat.

Grim was full of the joy of adventure. It seemed to him that the gods helped him to find his way through the dangerous coastal shallows; and he felt that they strengthened his arms to handle the heavy steering-sweep which was tied to the boat's starboard side. All through the night the boat was battered by fierce winds and swirling currents; but she passed safely along the winding channels and steered clear of wrecks and sandbanks. Grim stood tirelessly at the steering-sweep, forever singing his song; and his three sons took turns at pulling the oars and trimming the sail. Under the watchful eye of Grim's wife, Olaf lay wedged between the casks and slept peacefully.

When dawn broke above the cloud-capped mountains on the eastern shore of the Kattegat, Olaf awoke. Before he had time to feel sick or afraid, Grim's wife called him to help her serve food; and he served the men, as they worked the boat. Grim bobbed his head uneasily, when his King handed him a horn of ale; but Olaf liked serving these rough fishermen in their tiny boat on the fierce face of the vast, restless sea. He felt safer and happier than he had felt since his father was alive.

Olaf remembered little that his father had told him about England; but he remembered that it was a green land of low hills and lazy rivers; he remembered that his father had grown rich on English gold; and he remembered that it was many days' journey across the sea. He hugged himself happily; for England sounded comfortable and safe, far away from the terrors of Earl Thorard's camp. Soon Olaf joined in singing Grim's song, which rose and fell like the small boat; for the boat was always either climbing onto the top of a wave or sliding down, down, down into a trough.

On the second evening out they rounded the Skaw in the north of Denmark; and then they sailed southwestward down the Skaggerak towards England. Grim's two younger sons were pulling the pair of heavy oars amidships, to help the light wind in the sail; and Grim was pointing out the coast of Jutland, which was only a low green line on the horizon. Suddenly the look-out man, Grim's eldest son Knut, shouted "Ship ho!"

A boat lay dead ahead, right in the eye of the setting sun. The sea shone so brightly that they could not see what sort of boat she was. But she carried no sail; and there was no flash of dipping oar-blades. She lay on the sea like a lifeless log.

"They may be robbers lying in wait," Grim said. "Knut, strike the sail. Stop rowing portside."

Grim leant heavily on the steering-sweep; and the boat swung so suddenly to port that Olaf fell over. Knut gathered the yard, as it came crashing down in a flapping flurry of chequered cloth; and, by the time that he had stowed the sail, his two younger brothers were rowing strongly towards the land. Then Grim handed his wife the large steering-sweep and told her to steer for the far-away coast. Grim and Knut took two pair of longer, lighter oars; and they tied them into two pair of rowlocks in the narrow bow and stern of the boat; and soon three pair of oars were whipping the sea's sullen surface.

"Have they seen us?" Grim asked his wife, when all were pulling steadily; and she looked back over the starboard quarter.

"They must have seen us." she muttered and licked her lips in fear. "They have turned towards us; and I can see the splash of their oars."

"How many oars have they, wife?"

"I cannot see. But she is quite a big boat. I could see her length, as she came around."

"It is lucky that we were to windward of them when we saw them. Rowing into this swell will slow them down."

Grim's wife looked wild-eyed and anxious. But the four men set their teeth and pulled steadily and strongly; and they did not even raise their heads, to watch the other boat. Olaf saw nothing to be afraid of; but then he did not know that Norse robbers stole everything useful and sold all able-bodied prisoners as slaves; nor did he know that they often threw overboard whatever they did not want —such as young children. Olaf enjoyed the race; but he saw that the hunters would catch the hunted, long before the hunted could reach the shore.

Grim looked up at the sky. The sun had gone down in a glory of red and gold; but the bright colours of the sunset sky were being swallowed by dark storm-clouds spreading from the east. "The gods have sent rain. So pull, boys, pull." Grim shouted; and, pointing his chin, "Steer for the rain, wife," he added.

Olaf saw a thick curtain of misty rain hanging from the grey clouds to the grey sea. As the boat headed towards the rain, he jumped up and down with excitement. He looked astern, shading his eyes against the brightness of the western sky; and he watched the robbers' ten oared boat, like a big black beetle chasing them across the sparkling sea. Then he looked ahead. Beyond the bared teeth and hard shoulders of Grim and his sons the boat's beak bobbed up and down; and the pearly curtain of the rain crept towards them across the dark and sullen sea.

The hunters seemed much nearer than the misty rain; but suddenly "Phut!" a raindrop hit Olaf on the forehead. The choppy sea around the boat was dimpled, then flattened by a million steaming raindrops; and almost at once Olaf was wet through. When the robbers' boat was blotted from sight, Grim and his sons grinned in triumph; and, although the pitter-patter of rain grew louder, Olaf heard Grim's wife moaning with relief.

"We're not clear yet," Grim told her sternly. "Steer towards the land." Give her 10, boys!" he told his sons. "1, 2, 3, 4, 5, 6, 7, 8, 9, 10! Now rest and keep quiet."

The boat glided on in sudden silence, through the icy, chattering rain; but astern Olaf heard the rhythmic squawk of oars in their rowlocks, as the Norse robbers pulled on eastwards. Grim told his sons to muffle their oars with their shirts and to paddle lightly; and he told his wife at the steerboard to keep the brighter west on her right side. Although they often listened for their enemies, they reached the land without hearing anything.

Grim ran the boat into a tidal creek and hid her among the reeds; and they slept that night huddled damply together under the sail in the bottom of the boat. Next morning the rain had gone. But they did not dare to hoist the sail, for fear that the robbers might see it; and they paddled along close inshore, with a good look-out seawards. Luckily they never saw the robbers' boat again; and soon they were out of the Skagerrak and into the open sea.

Olaf was often hungry and thirsty and cold during the ten days' voyage to the English coast; but in spite of that he was as happy as a lark and sang Grim's song from morning to night. The men were all tired with working the boat; but they bobbed their heads respectfully to the skinny little King-born, whenever he brought them food or drink. Olaf heard Grim say: "Other Danes have met storms and head winds on the crossing to England. But the gods must love our little King; for we have met no storms and have had fair winds all the way. Let us hope that the gods will save us from the English too; for we shall be strangers in their land; and they do not love the Danes."

One morning they saw ahead of them a green line on the horizon. When they came closer, they saw grassy cliffs on their starboard bow; and, ahead of them and stretching away to port, they saw a saltmarsh with low hills behind it. But the cliffs turned out to be a headland; and behind the headland there was a wide river with tidal marshes along both its banks.

"Glory be to Mighty Magnus and all the other gods!" Grim cried, "for this must be the River Humber. The gods have guided us so well" he said: "that I leave it to them to make a good landing." But, to let the gods know just what was wanted, he went on loudly: "We need a lonely place, where we can be safe against attack. We need firm earth, on which to build our hut, and still water, in which to moor our boat. We need to be near good fishing-grounds and also near towns or camps where we can sell our fish."

With the gods' help, Grim landed on the right bank of the River Humber, near its mouth; and there he built a small hall on a hillock. Fishermen have lived there ever since—at Grimsby.

CHAPTER IV

THE KITCHEN BOY

The gods had guarded Grim's small boat on the long voyage over the sea from Denmark; they had guided him to make his new home on a hill among the fens beside the River Humber; and they smiled on Grim and the people of Grimsby during Olaf's childhood.

Grim's fishing-nets were always full; and he did well by selling his fish. He built new boats and enlarged his hall. His sons married, had children, and built halls for themselves. Every year more Danes fled from Denmark, where the greedy Thorard had made himself King. Grimsby became a large and wealthy village; but Grim remained its headman.

Olaf King-born grew up as a fisherboy. The other Danes in Grimsby wished to serve him as their King; but he took his turn at the nets and oars; and he carried Grim's fish in big, plaited baskets to farms and monasteries nearby. Often he carried fish to the town of Louth and to shepherds on the windy Wolds;

and sometimes he carried his baskets of fish right over the Wolds to the rich English towns on the River Trent.

Whatever Olaf did, he never forgot his father's last words: 'Olaf shall be King, when he can put the weight further than Thorard and can throw him at the wrestling.' He put the weight daily; and he took on all comers at wrestling. By the time that he was fifteen, he was bigger and stronger than anyone in Grimsby; and that year he won the Grimsby Games, which each year marked the day of Grim's arrival.

As soon as Olaf had won the Grimsby Games, Grim's good luck changed. From that day on Grim thought himself lucky to catch a single fish; and, to make matters worse, a very bad harvest and an early autumn made corn and meat dear. The fishermen of Grimsby no longer caught enough to feed their families. So Olaf, who ate a lot, made up his mind to go to Lincoln to earn his own living.

Grim could not give Olaf a tunic, a mantle and stockings of woollen cloth, such as English townsmen usually wore; but he gave him an old red boat-cover; and from the faded red canvas Grim's wife made Olaf a short mantle and a knee-length tunic. "Canvas is not the cloth for kings," Olaf said, "but, when I sleep out under the thorn-bushes, my mantle must be my roof against the October rain." Then the King-born set out for Lincoln like a barefoot beggar.

At that time Lincoln was one of the largest towns in England. The wooden houses were crowded higgledy-piggledy in and around the walls; and, because five thousand people lived there without drains, the town stank and flies were everywhere. But Olaf thought that the high stone gateways and the neat stone walls built by the Romans seven hundred years earlier were very splendid; and he gaped with wonder to see a tall church also built of stone; for he had never seen a stone building.

Olaf asked for work from door to door. But he could find nobody who would give him even one meal for a whole day's work. So he slept in the bushes outside the town and went hungry. The next day was the same; for people were starving that year, even before the winter had begun. Many lean and ragged men were begging for bread and eating scraps thrown out for the dogs. But the King-born was too proud to beg or fight dogs. So he went hungry again.

On the third day Olaf's hungry belly awakened him long before sunrise; and he went to Wigford wharf, beside the River Witham and outside the South Gate of Lincoln town. Many hungry beggars were there before him, helping to unload vegetables and other goods from the river-boats; for they hoped to get a handful of beans or a crust of bread for their work. Olaf could find no one who would let him work; but suddenly he heard a faraway shout: "Porters! Porters! Porters wanted here!"

With desperate eagerness all the beggars ran; and the man who had called was already surrounded by twenty ragged, scraggy men, when Olaf reached him. That big boy did not wait behind the crowd. He jumped upon the back of one scrawny beggar; and he crawled over the heads of the rest, until he was looking down at a large, bald man. Among the starving, half-naked beggars the bald man seemed rich; for he was not only large but also fat; and he wore a cowled cloak and long stockings of good brown cloth and a tunic of Lincoln green.

"I need two porters for these two baskets." the large man was saying.

"Not so, master!" Olaf shouted loudly. "I can carry both those baskets myself."

The man was surprised to see a young giant lying on the heads of the crowd. "Mountain ox," he joked, "you shall have the task." But he warned him sternly: "If you drop my goods, I shall beat you so hard that you will be unable to lift anything for a week."

Olaf thrust aside his starving rivals and took a basket in each hand. He followed the bald man over the bridge; and, when the man got on his horse, Olaf followed the horse. He walked behind the horse right through Lincoln, toiling up the steep hill towards the church and castle at the top. By the time that he came to the top of the hill, his muscles were aching; but he sang Grim's song, to show that he still had plenty of breath left.

The bald man was the steward of Lincoln Castle; and Olaf's baskets held food for the King's Reeve and his spearmen. For Lincoln Castle belonged to the King of England; and the Reeve and his men lived in the castle and guarded the King's rights in the shire of Lindsey. The English kings had built a "burgh" inside the stone wall of the old Roman castrum; and the steward led Olaf through the Roman gate and then over the ditch and through a log fence.

Olaf found that the burgh was rather like his father's camp; for it was circular; and its defences were made of timber and earth but it was very much smaller and more haphazard than the vast and well-planned Danish war-camps. However, squared stones had been filched from the Roman walls, to build a lofty hall in the middle. The Reeve's hall was even higher and longer than the fine stone church outside the castle wall. Stone buildings seemed very splendid to Olaf; and he thought that the King of England must be very rich.

The steward dismounted outside the hall; but he did not climb the stone steps. Instead he entered a round wooden hut, shaped like a beehive, which stood near the hall. When Olaf followed, he saw that this hut was a kitchen; and with a happy sigh he put his muddy, bloody baskets on the round tree-trunk which served as a table.

"Not there, you lout!" the steward roared. "Put them on the ground."

"Sorry, master! I will clean your board at once," the King-born said humbly; and he wiped the table with his own red mantle.

"That is better," said the steward and handed him a quarter of a silver penny. "Here is your farthing. If you come to the wharf tomorrow morning, perhaps I shall have another task for you."

"At what time will you be there, master?"

"At the same time as today! I like to buy my food before the sun warms it."

"I shall be there, master; and tomorrow I shall be able to carry more; for this silver will buy me some food today."

"Did you not eat yesterday?" the steward asked.

"No, master! Nor the day before that! But now I shall buy myself a big loaf of bread, to fill my empty belly."

"Wait, boy! Wait, till I find some broth for you," the kindly steward said; and he ladled some soup from a large iron pot hanging over the fire. "Drink this bowl of hot broth, boy. I do not want your flesh to melt from your bones before tomorrow morning."

Olaf drank the soup and thanked the steward. Then he went to the market outside the castle gate and bought himself a large loaf of bread. With his belly full again, he felt sure that his luck had changed; and, singing his song, he set out to find more work as a porter. But, while he was walking down the steep hill towards the river, he heard a cry of alarm and looked around. A runaway horse was clattering down the street towards him, with two baskets of goods bouncing on its sides, Olaf jumped out and caught the runaway's rein; and, although the horse struggled wildly, he held on and stopped it.

"You again!" cried the horse's owner, when he reached Olaf; for it was the castle steward. "So you are a stable-boy as well as a porter, eh?" he joked and gave Olaf another farthing. "I will watch out for you at the river-market tomorrow morning, boy. But in these bad days I cannot give you work, unless you get to me among the first. So do not be late," the steward warned Olaf, as they parted.

Next morning, even before the first light of day had streaked the eastern sky with silver-grey, Olaf went to the wharf. He looked for boats unloading sheep; for the previous day he had met the steward buying meat. But he could find no meat at all; and so he waited near the vegetable-boats, wondering what the steward would do without meat. The clouds were already dusted with rosy pink, before the steward came striding over the humpbacked bridge; and to Olaf's dismay the steward went off to another part of the wharf. Olaf ran after the steward and found him standing beside the fishing-boats. Olaf was very surprised that such a great man should want to eat poor fishermen's food; for he thought that even the toughest meat tasted better than fish. But he bowed low.

"You need not call for porters today, master. I myself will carry all that you can buy," he boasted.

"You have not yet seen how much fish I shall buy," the steward pointed out. "Today is fish-Friday; and my men need to eat twice as much fish as they do meat. It will be a heavy load."

The steward bought one basketful of herring, halibut, skate and plaice for the spearmen; and then

45

he bought a second basketful of salmon, cuttlefish, eels and lampreys for the Reeve's own table. So Olaf already had a basket under each arm, as he followed the steward to the vegetable-boats; and there the steward bought six large cabbages, a sack of beans and a big bag of dried peas. Olaf put down the baskets of fish, while he packed the vegetables into a third basket; and then he waited for the steward to move on. But, with a mocking grin, the steward stood staring at the three heavy baskets.

"Is that all, master?" Olaf asked uneasily.

"That is all, boy. But have you a third hand? Or must I after all call another porter?" the steward mocked him.

"If you will lend me the leading-rein from your horse, master, I can carry one basket on my back." Olaf suggested.

"That is so, boy. But my horse is at the city gate beyond the bridge. Do you expect ME to carry a basket over the bridge?" the steward asked in a ferocious voice.

"Oh no, master!" Olaf said meekly.

The steward shrugged his shoulders and winked knowingly at the vegetable-seller. Then he turned and walked quickly along the wharf and over the high bridge towards his horse. But, when he turned at the top of the bridge to watch Olaf juggling his three baskets, he cried out in surprise. For Olaf was following close behind and almost breathing down his neck. The burly boy was carrying one basket in each arm; and the third basket was balanced on his cloak, which was folded on top of his head.

"Now that is very clever, young fellow. Where did you learn to carry a basket on your head?" the steward asked.

"I have been doing that for years, master. If I have to go far with two baskets, I always carry one on my back and the other on my head. I have often carried fish from Grimsby to Louth in that way."

"From Grimsby to Louth? That is a long way to carry two baskets of fish. No wonder that you are strong!"

When they had reached the castle kitchen and Olaf had put his baskets down, the steward asked, "Do you know how to scale fish and to skin eels, boy?"

"Yes, master! I was brought up as a fisherman."

"Then why are you working as a porter so far from the sea?" the steward demanded.

"Alas, master! The fish have swum away from Grimsby; and this summer we could not catch enough to feed us. So I left my family and came to Lincoln, to find other work."

The steward was thoughtful. "Then clean these fish for the pot," he said. "If you do it well, you can stay here and work in my kitchen. I like strong men about me. I am getting fat now; but, when I was younger, I was a champion strongman," he explained. He looked at Olaf's well-muscled arms and legs. Then he nodded.

"I think that you also could be good at games," he said, "for you have a well-made body. When you have cleaned those fish, boy, I will teach you the manly sport of putting the weight."

The steward was amazed at the distance which Olaf could put the weight. But he showed the boy a better way to hold the round stone; and he made him heave the weight with his legs as well as with his arms and shoulders. Then Olaf was amazed; for he had thrown the weight five feet further than ever before.

Let me see how far YOU can throw the stone, King-born, he heard his wicked uncle's voice. "Just wait awhile; and you SHALL see, traitor," Olaf whispered; and, gritting his teeth, he threw the stone again and again, until he could hardly stand.

CHAPTER V

THE GREAT GAMES

From that day Olaf, the big, handsome boy, and Master Eric, the big, fat steward, became fast friends; but the low-born steward gave all the orders; and the King-born youth obeyed him. For Olaf was only the kitchen-boy. He drew and fetched water from the well; he chopped and carried logs and kindling wood; he cleaned the hearth and spread rushes on the floor of the hall; he plucked fowls and skinned meat, scaled fish and peeled eels, watched pots and turned the spit.

As payment for his work Olaf was fed once a day and clothed once a year. To the steward's surprise his kitchen-boy ate as much as four spearmen. For Olaf, who was already very tall and still building muscle, always remembered Thorard's scornful advice: "Eat well, King-born, or you will never grow strong enough to beat me." Olaf meant to beat Earl Thorard when he was full-grown; and he put the weight, tossed the pine-log and practised wrestling, whenever

49

he could. Whatever Thorard had said, he WAS going to be "King Olaf the Strong."

Master Eric often joined Olaf at his games in the castle-yard. The kindly steward had no idea that Olaf was a king's son; but he knew that Olaf could be a champion strongman. He prayed God to guide him in training the boy well; and he made sure that his pupil was eating enough body building food and going to sleep early. Master Eric worked so hard to train young Olaf that he melted his own fat and lifted his belly back into his chest. The people of Lincoln often came to the castle, to watch the two strongmen, the cunning old baldy and his golden-haired pupil.

The King's Reeve in Lindsey was a well-born English thane called Harald Eldredson. He was tall, with thick grey hair, long moustaches and a forked beard; and in his youth he had been a famous warrior. One day, when Thane Harald came home from hunting, he watched Olaf wrestling. "Who is that big boy?" he asked the steward. Eric told the Thane as much of Olaf's story as he knew; and he said that Olaf was now working in the castle kitchen.

"A big fellow like him ought to be a warrior rather than a kitchen-boy," the Thane decided. "You can teach him wrestling and the other games of strength; but I myself will train him in the noble art of arms."

So on weekdays Olaf learned sporting skill from one old champion and the use of arms from another; and for three years he grew in size, skill, strength and beauty. People gasped with wonder, when first they saw the handsome, golden-haired youth stripped to the waist; and the townsmen would wait for hours, to watch him fighting with the six foot staff or wrestling against two men. But that was on weekdays. On Sundays and feast days Olaf shaved and went with the steward's family to the stone church beside the castle; and for the first time in his life he became a good Christian.

Olaf was well liked in Lincoln. For one reason, he was the largest and strongest man in the town; and in those days people admired size and strength more than anything else except courage. For another reason, he was always cheerful and good-tempered. For a third reason, he was always willing to help other people and to play with the children. For a fourth reason, he was neither greedy nor even clever; and therefore no one needed to be afraid of him.

One spring day, when Olaf was eighteen, he was called to the hall. The Reeve was sitting on his oak chest opposite the hearth-stone, and beside him stood the steward. Both of them looked very solemn.

"Olaf the kitchen-boy!" the Reeve said gravely. "I have had you taught all the skills both of manly games and of handling arms. Now the time has come when you must repay me for all my work and care."

"I will do anything, Lord," Olaf said at once, "not only to pay my debt for your lessons but also for love, Lord. You, Lord, have been like an uncle to me; and Master Eric has been like a father."

"So you think that the King's Reeve and his low-born steward are BROTHERS?" the noble Thane snorted. But, when he looked at the guileless face of his handsome, hulking kitchen-boy, his frown faded; and he said grudgingly, "Perhaps we ARE brothers in our love of manly strength and skill."

"Only tell me, Lord, what I can do for you; and, with God's help, I will do it," Olaf said humbly.

The Reeve stroked his moustache and beard, cleared his throat and spat a gob into the empty brazier which stood on the hearth-stone. Then he pierced Olaf with his sharp blue eyes.

"In a fortnight's time the Great Summer Games will be held before the Lord King at Stamford," he said. "And you must try your strength and skill. There will be wrestling and pitching the pine-log, putting the weight and fighting with the staff, throwing the spear and splitting the willow-wand.

52

The steward and I have taught you the skills of all these games. But, Olaf, you can beat the best men in England, only if you yourself have the heart of a hero. When a man is bone weary, only his heart's courage can give him strength; and, when he is near defeat, only the fiery soul of a true champion can light the way to victory. Did your fisherman father give you those great gifts?" he asked Olaf doubtfully.

Olaf was reminded of King Magnus' dying words.

"Lord, a hero's blood runs in my veins," he said proudly, "and a champion's soul burns in my breast." But tears started from his eyes; and, in order to hide his face, he bowed his head onto his master's knees. "I will try to do you honour, Lord," he mumbled.

During the next two weeks Olaf was driven mercilessly by his teachers; and he was on the move, working like an ox or practising for the Games, for all the daylight hours. But, when it was dark, he was called into the warm kitchen. There he was rubbed down with a coarse cloth, to chase life-giving blood through his tired muscles; and he was fed with slabs of red meat and a wooden bowl of five day ale. Then he was sent to bed.

The Reeve told his tailor to make new clothes for Olaf to wear to the Mayday Games; and before daybreak on the last day of April Olaf put them on.

First he put on a shirt and drawers of white linen. Next he pulled on coarse, red-and-white speckled stockings and tied them to the string of his drawers. Then he cross-gartered the hairy stockings with strips of yellow cloth; and over them he bound black felt shoes. Finally he pushed his head into a green cloth tunic and wrapped himself around with a blue cloth mantle. Olaf saw that the hems of both tunic and mantle were finely embroidered with red and yellow wool. Never in his life, even as a Danish prince, had Olaf King-born been so well dressed.

At dawn Olaf mounted a peaceable nag; and, with Thane Harald, Master Eric the Steward and a guard of twenty spearmen, he set out to ride the forty miles to Stamford. They slept that night in Grantham at the house of a kinsman of the Reeve; and early on May Morning they rode on to Stamford.

Stamford was crowded. Lords and ladies, farmers and warriors, great earls and beggars, Christians and heathens jostled one another; and the narrow streets were further blocked by sheep and cattle, carts and traders' stalls. The Reeve's spearmen often had to wield their long spear-staves, in order to reach the field of the Games; and the field itself was so crowded that Olaf did not believe that the Great Games could be held there.

Olaf and his masters left their horses and weapons with Thane Harald's guard outside the field; for weapons were forbidden at the Games. Then on foot the three men forced their way through the crowd into the middle of the field.

Coming towards them from the opposite side of the crowded field Olaf saw a wedge of spears and helmets. Three hundred spearmen were clearing a path through the unarmed crowd. Olaf thought that only a VERY great man would dare to bring an armed guard into the sacred place. "Here comes the King," Thane Harald cried and waved his little cap. A large band of men and women were walking their horses through the path cleared by the spearmen. In front rode the King. His red hair bushed out beneath a gold crown; his waxed red moustaches were as wide as his ears; and a forked red beard nearly hid his chest. He wore a long mantle of blue cloth trimmed with beaver fur over a long, split tunic of embroidered blue silk; and his shoes, his girdle and the straps which cross-gartered his scarlet woollen stockings were of gilded leather. But with every step of his horse he clinked; for he never dared to leave his own hall without his mail shirt; and his sword hung ever-ready at his side.

Behind the King a young girl was sitting sideways on a led horse. She had green eyes; and red-gold hair hung in two heavy plaits from under her head-veil. Her veil and her gown were made of silk the colour of ivory; her overtunic was of scarlet cloth bordered with gold braid and tied round the waist with a golden cord; and her hip-length mantle was made of blue cloth trimmed with beaver. *As pretty as the pictures in Lincoln Cathedral!* Olaf thought as he stared; but Thane Harald pulled at his arm and led him to an open space cleared by the spearmen. Pages were setting a chest for the King and benches for his family; and the strongmen who wanted to try their luck were already gathering in front of the seats.

Olaf stood on the edge of the open space and watched the big, bearded men who were his rivals. They flexed their muscles and blew out their cheeks; and they tried the feel of the weight, the pine-log, the spear and the staves, which had been put ready for the Mayday Games. Olaf gazed in wonder at these huge and hairy men; but, when Thane Harald went to greet the King, he found himself staring at the red-haired girl; and he stared at her so long and so hard that the sudden sound of the herald's horn made him jump.

The Master of the Games stepped into the open space in front of the King and sang out: "Hear ye! Hear ye the King's will! All those strongmen who wish to take part in the Great Games must prove their strength in putting the weight. Stand forward, all you strongmen."

Twenty big men stepped forward with Olaf; and each man's name was clearly written by the King's chaplain on a large wooden peg. The pegs were then stuck into the ground in a line before the King. One by one the strongmen were called to throw the heavy, round stone called "the weight;" and each man's peg was stuck into the ground where his stone had landed. But Master Eric mocked their clumsiness. "These men have no more skill than oxen," he whispered to Olaf.

Suddenly Olaf heard his own name called. He pulled his tunic and shirt over his head; and, wearing only his baggy white drawers, wrinkled red stockings and black felt shoes, he walked forward to take the stone. He heard a sudden buzz of excited chatter; for some people asked who this new fellow was; and others said scornfully that no one had ever seen a strongman with milk-white skin and a beardless chin. A moment later there was a loud gasp of surprise. For Olaf crouched; and then he sprang, as the steward had taught him; and he threw the weight six feet further than anyone who had yet thrown.

Nevertheless, as Olaf took his shirt from Master Eric, he shook his head glumly. "I did not do it right, master," he said. "I left the throw too late."

"Never mind, boy! You have two more throws; and no one can walk out in front of the King and throw his best the very first time. Next time don't hurry; and you will do better," the old champion advised his young pupil.

Olaf turned to look at the red-headed girl. But he dropped his eyes at once; for she was already staring at him. At that moment Master Eric whispered urgently, "Watch this man, Olaf. He is the Earl Leowulf, a mighty warrior and lord of East Anglia. He is also a famous strongman; and he has won the May Games for the past four years."

Leowulf was a giant— a good foot taller than Olaf and broader too. He had wavy black hair and a long black beard; and, when he stripped off his green silk tunic and white linen shirt, Olaf saw that his back, chest and belly were also hairy. Proudly Leowulf walked out into the open space, swinging his long arms and rolling the muscles in his back and shoulders. He picked up the big stone as easily as though it was a small loaf of bread; and he spun it around in his fingers. Then suddenly he dipped his shoulder and threw the stone two feet beyond Olaf s peg.

When Olaf threw again, he passed Leowulf s peg by a few inches; but he told Master Eric with a worried frown, "Again I did it badly. I got the spring; I got the shoulder-roll; and I got the snap of the elbow. But I did not get them all together."

"Do not worry, boy. You have another throw," the steward pointed out. "Take your time; and give your whole mind as well as your body to that last throw."

None of the others threw the stone as far as the two leaders; but Leowulf at his second throw heaved the weight three feet past Olaf s peg. Olaf thought that he had little chance of bettering Leowulf's throw; but, as he was walking out for his third throw, he glanced at the red-haired girl sitting behind the King. She was gazing at him with anxious eyes; and her fists were pressed against her mouth. Olaf could see that she wanted him to win; and he set his teeth and thrust out his jaw. It had suddenly become very important that he should please her.

For a time Olaf stood, tossing the round stone from hand to hand and staring at the ground. He was gathering together all Master Eric's advice and concentrating his mind and body on the throw. Then he raised his eyes to the sky and silently prayed his father to fan the flames of kingship burning in his breast. Lastly he filled his lungs and blew upon the stone, to warm it with the gods' breath.

Like a man under a spell, Olaf stepped to the line.

He crouched. Then he sprang; and, as he sprang, he swivelled his shoulders; and he flung out his arm with a snap of the elbow. In a single, flowing movement of graceful power he hurled the weight. The great stone flew far beyond Leowulf's mark and far beyond any throw which Olaf had ever made.

While cheering roared and bellowed in his ears, Olaf stumbled like a sleep-walker back to his place.

"With the help of all the gods in heaven, everything went right that time." Olaf whispered to Master Eric, who was moist-eyed with pride at his pupil's success. As Olaf was pulling his shirt on over his head, he staggered beneath a great thump on the back. He turned in surprise and was swallowed by the hug of black-bearded Leowulf, who shouted generously: "Well done! Well done! Never have I seen such a throw."

No other strongman reached the marks of Olaf and Leowulf; and, when Leowulf was called for his third throw, he stood by Olaf's side and shouted: "I shall not fight against the will of the gods. In truth I am proud to be second to a throw like Olaf's; and I dare swear that no mortal man will ever match that throw, unless it is Olaf the Strong himself. Let your clerks measure and write down the length of that throw," he told the King. "For men in later years ought to read in the chronicle of your reign the true distance of that mighty throw; and your grandchildren should pace it out on the ground and rejoice that this wondrous feat of strength was done in your presence."

The King just nodded. But the red-haired girl sitting behind him was hugging herself with delight; and her grey-green eyes sparkled like the sun-drenched sea, as she smiled at Olaf.

CHAPTER VI

THE STRONGEST MAN IN ENGLAND

The King's clerks cut three notches in Olaf's scoring-peg; and they put two notches in Leowulf's peg. They also cut a notch for one Beorn, who was shaped like a barrel and almost covered in matted red hair: for he had been third in the weightputting.

After sounding his horn, the Master of the Games called the strongmen to an archery contest. A peeled willow-wand was stuck into the ground; and from fifty paces away each man shot at the stick, until he had split it. Olaf split the stick with his third arrow; but Leowulf did it with his second arrow. At the spear-throwing Leowulf threw furthest; and Olaf was again second. At pitching the pine-log they tied for first place.

The king's clerks counted the notches scored on each man's peg; and they replanted in the ground before the King only those four pegs which had been scored the most. Then the herald called on the four best men to fight with staves.

First, Leowulf was summoned to fight a dark-skinned, hairy man, who was almost as broad as he was long. Leowulf tricked the man into hitting out wildly; and, when the dark man lost his balance, Leowulf thwacked his head to win the bout. The dark man's peg was thrown away; and for a moment Leowulf's peg stood alone, while the priests were reading the names on the other two pegs.

"Beorn, the Brampton Bear, and Olaf, the young Dane!" the herald shouted; and the big, barrel-shaped, redhaired man stepped out, grinning confidently.

"Do not be afraid of this hairy Bear." Thane Harald whispered to his pupil Olaf. "He has not got the skill that you have. Let him slash at you and lose his balance. Then hook his leg and throw him over."

As Olaf took his staff, he again caught the eye of the red-haired girl; and it made him over-eager, so that he slipped on a patch of mud and fell on one knee. The Bear attacked fiercely; but Olaf skillfully parried a hail of slashing blows, as he got to his feet. At last Olaf drooped, as though he was tired; and he lowered his staff and left his head unguarded.

The Bear saw his chance; and he leapt upon Olaf, with his staff swinging. But Olaf quickly dropped into a crouch and ducked under the Bear's slash. Then he pushed his staff between the Bear's legs and hooked his ankle. He heaved the Bear upside-down onto his nose; and, while the Bear sprawled on the ground, he tapped him on the head for victory.

The black-robed clerks jostled one another to reach the pegs. Like a hawk's taloned foot, a thin white hand shot out from its long black sleeve. In a trice the Bear of Brampton's peg was plucked from the earth and cast into the crowd. Now only two pegs stood fast —Leowulf's and Olaf's.

Olaf glanced shyly at the shining face of the red-haired girl. Then he dropped his eyes and walked quietly back to his masters. Thane Harald was hammering his right fist into his left hand, saying: "I knew he could do it. I knew he could do it." But, whatever he said, the noble Thane seemed unable to believe in his pupil's triumph. Master Eric, however, was already thinking about the next contest.

"Now for the wrestling!" he said seriously. "That will not be so easy. For Earl Leowulf is not like the Bear, just brute strength and brutish ignorance. He is a skillful wrestler, very skillful indeed, and very strong too. But you have one thing which Earl

Leowulf has already lost, Olaf; and that is youth. By now Leowulf must be more than thirty years old; and, for all his big bones and mighty muscles, there is a roll of blubber bulging over his girdle. I believe that Leowulf cannot last for long at full strength. You must make him do as much work as you can at the start of the fight.

Soon he will become a little slower and a little softer. Then speed up your attacks and try to throw him by using his own weight. But avoid his bear-hug; or you'll be finished. May God be with you, boy!"

When Olaf was called, he pulled off his shirt and started forward; but Master Eric held him by the arm and reminded him in a whisper:

"Don't forget to use his own weight to throw him down."

Olaf and Leowulf walked to the middle of the ring in front of the King; and, as they went, they tightened the girdles of their linen drawers. Olaf now saw that, as Master Eric had said, Leowulf had a roll of fat bulging over his girdle. The two strongmen bowed to the king. Then on a sudden whim Olaf bowed also to the red-haired girl; but he was surprised when Leowulf bowed to her. *Perhaps she is the King's daughter,* he thought; but the King scowled angrily; and Olaf was puzzled and uneasy.

"Before we use our strength in an effort to become the strongmen's King, Olaf, let us swear to be friends forever." Leowulf said cheerfully, as he held out his hands. The brown-skinned, black-haired giant and the fair-skinned, golden boy held each other's wrists in the middle of the ring; and the onlookers cheered, as the two big, handsome men smiled at each other.

The Master of the Games sounded his horn and cried on high: "Hear ye! Hear ye the King's will! The last game to decide who shall be 'The King of the Strongmen of England' is three bouts of wrestling. The first to win two bouts shall be the winner. Stand forth the Earls of Mercia and of Kent, to judge the fairness of the falls."

The two wrestlers crouched with their hands spread; and, when the judges gave the signal, Olaf and Leowulf sprang upon each other. Sometimes they were locked together chest to chest like two bears; sometimes one would twist an arm or leg or would throw the other bodily across the grass; but most of the time they circled warily, looking for an opening.

Olaf kept always in mind Master Eric's advice. He made Leowulf do the greater part of the hard work; and, whenever he could, he made use of Leowulf's own weight to throw him off-balance. When Leowulf strained to throw Olaf down, Olaf would suddenly throw himself the same way; and, while Leowulf stumbled to keep his feet, Olaf would roll and wriggle out of his grasp.

"Ah! You are as slippery as a fish." Leowulf cried, when he had lost Olaf for the tenth time.

"Not a fish but a fisher!" Olaf replied. "For I am a fisherman by trade."

"Then come and catch me, you Danish fisherman. Or are you only a Viking thief?" sneered Leowulf.

That made Olaf angry; and for a moment he forgot Master Eric's advice. He rushed at Leowulf, to throw him by main force. But Leowulf hugged Olaf to his strong chest and lifted Olaf's feet from the ground. Then Leowulf threw himself down; and, as they fell on the grass, he rolled on top of Olaf and pinned his shoulders to the earth.

"One fall to Earl Leowulf!" the judges cried.

Olaf had learnt his lesson; and in the second bout he made Leowulf reach out for him and fumble for a grip. As the bout went on and on, Olaf could feel the strength oozing out of Leowulf's muscles. Leowulf's movements became slower; and his flesh felt softer. But Olaf did not dare to match his strength against that of the gigantic Leowulf.

Olaf danced and darted around Leowulf, now pulling his arm, now tripping his ankle. But at last

Leowulf got a hold on Olaf's shoulders and tried to throw him. Olaf braced himself against the throw, until Leowulf had put all his weight into it. Then, suddenly doubling his legs beneath him, Olaf tumbled like a ball; and he dragged big Leowulf with him, over him, under him, and held him down, until the judges shouted: "One fall to Olaf!" and Leowulf panted: "Well done, fisherman!"

From then on both wrestlers knew that, barring accident or folly, Olaf would win. His white skin was red with the mauling of Leowulf's fingers; but Leowulf's age had begun to show. The muscles of his panting chest and belly sagged with weariness; and his eyes peered bloodshot from beneath black brows running with sweat.

However, Olaf still needed to throw the huge man and to hold him down; and Leowulf's jutting jaw showed that he would fight with all his strength and all his skill until the judges shouted, "Fall!"

Olaf feigned weariness and left himself unguarded, in order to encourage Leowulf to attack him; but Leowulf only grunted, "You cannot trick me with that sort of game, you Danish puppy. You must come and get me."

Then Olaf remembered how in the first bout he had been angered by Leowulf's taunts; and he remembered how, when he rushed rashly in, Leowulf had hugged him to his chest and had thrown him to the ground. Now he scowled angrily, to encourage Leowulf to taunt him again; and soon Leowulf stood back with his hands on his hips and gave a scornful laugh. "Unless you come and get me, milk-skinned girl, you will have to wait until I lie down." Leowulf sneered. "But I shall not lie down before bedtime, pretty lady," he bellowed.

Olaf roared with rage and rushed at Leowulf, with chest raised and arms outstretched to grasp his shoulders; and Leowulf eagerly swayed forward, to meet the charge upon his chest. But Olaf ducked under Leowulf's deadly embrace. He clasped Leowulf's knees against his shoulders and forced the legs upwards and backwards. Then he twisted the huge body, as it fell. Leowulf landed heavily on his back; and Olaf dropped on him like a hawk.

The black-haired giant kicked and struggled, as he tried to roll over; but he was too tired to push Olaf off him. Both the judges and all the people shouted, "Olaf is the winner."

Leowulf clasped Olaf to his chest.

"Ah! You lovely knave!" he said with a chuckle. "I meant to stay on my feet till dark rather than give you an opening for your twisting and tumbling. But you made a fool of me, golden man. You made a fool of me."

Master Eric helped Olaf up; and then Olaf pulled at Leowulf's great weight, to raise him to his feet. But, pull as he would, he could hardly raise the laughing giant's shoulders from the ground.

"You see, my friend, that I am more easily put down than raised up. For I am an earl who will never be a king." Leowulf said with a wink.

Olaf did not understand what Leowulf meant; and it was only several hours later that he found out.

When the two wrestlers had put on their clothes and combed their hair, they were led to the King's seat. As they bent the knee, the herald stood forth, to cry the winner; but Leowulf himself boomed out the news in a voice like a great church bell. "The King of the Strongmen of England," he cried, "is Olaf the Dane."

Leowulf told the King: "Like a good fisherman, Olaf has trapped a shaggy red bear and landed a fat black whale. Perhaps," Leowulf went on, "his nimble wrestling and his speed with the staff may soon be forgotten; but, Lord King, I dare swear that men will long remember Olaf's weightput; for that was made in the house of the Danish Gods by Thor the Thunderer himself. Ahhh!" he cried, raising both his hands to heaven, "that was a throw the like of which has never been seen in England."

Mindful of his royal duty, the King held his hand out towards Olaf; and Olaf touched the hand to his forehead. "Where do you come from, strongman?" the King asked. But he yawned openly; for these peasants' games bored him. He was a warrior born and bred.

"As a child, Lord King, I came from Denmark; and for a while I was a fisherman at Grimsby." Olaf answered. "But now I live in your burgh at Lincoln; and there I work as a kitchen-boy."

The King's face came alive; and he laughed aloud. "A KITCHEN-boy! The strongest man in England!" he mocked Olaf; and he asked the crowd, "Who would ever have thought of a joke like that?" Then, hoping to make fun of a simpleton, he asked, "Where is this Grimsby, where your father lives? I have never heard of it."

"My father died in Denmark, when I was a small boy," Olaf answered calmly. "It is my foster-father, the fisherman Grim, who lives at Grimsby, which is a fishing village on the southern bank of the River Humber."

The red-haired girl had left her bench, to stand beside the King; and, when the King saw the eagerness in her face, he smiled scornfully. "The Lady Goldenburg, my ward, shows you favour, kitchen-boy," he said and looked down his nose. "The Noble Lady has been much pleased by your sweaty labours."

The red-haired girl held her hand towards Olaf, as he knelt on the grass; and he touched it humbly to his forehead. Then, while he grasped her small, soft hand with his large, horny fingers, he gazed deep into her grey-green eyes.

"If my throw was made by the Thunder God, Lady, he must have forged it in the fire of YOUR eyes," he blurted out.

"I am glad, Olaf Dane," the little lady answered. "I wanted you to win. Earl Leowulf has been King of the Strongmen for long enough; and I am pleased to see a golden-haired champion among the reds and blacks."

Olaf stared into the Lady Goldenburg's eyes, as though he was a rabbit hypnotised by a stoat. He was too dazed to let go her hand; and she did not withdraw it. But suddenly the King slapped his knees, as though he had just thought of something good, and jumped to his feet.

"Come, child," he said cheerfully. "The sun is low in the sky; and we must not be caught out of doors in the dark. However, you may meet your King of the Strongmen one of these days, when we go to

Lincoln." The King turned away with a sly smile; but the Lady Goldenburg said quietly to Olaf, "May God protect you, Olaf the Strong! I shall ask my guardian to take me to Lincoln soon, so that I can have a longer talk with you."

"Noble lady, I thank you for your favour; but remember that I am only a kind of kitchen-boy," Olaf said humbly.

"King of the Strongmen," whispered the Lady, "remember that I am only a kind of captive queen."

CHAPTER VII

A KIND OF CAPTIVE QUEEN

A kind of captive queen. What does that mean? Olaf asked himself, as the Lady Goldenburg walked quickly away after the King. But his thoughts were broken by a hand on his shoulder and Thane Harald's voice.

"Wake up! Wake up, King of the Strongmen! The great Earl Leowulf has asked us to be his guests at Crowland, which is a few miles down the river; and we must start at once, to reach it before dark."

Olaf did not like to ask his master, Thane Harald, what the Lady Goldenburg had meant by her words; for he knew that Harald was the King's man; and he felt that the King was in some way an enemy of the Lady Goldenburg. So he kept his questions to himself, as he followed the Thane and Master Eric to the horses; and he said nothing, when they joined Earl Leowulf and his gang of thanes and hearthmen.

As they left Stamford, the talk was of the Games and of the strongmen who had taken part. But after a few miles Olaf found that Leowulf was riding beside him; and he saw that Leowulf's men were talking busily to his own masters. Leowulf slowed his horse, to point out to Olaf where the old Roman road called "King Street" forded a river at Deeping. The road was only a ridge of earth and stone between ditches; but in the slanting sunlight its shadow cut straight across the flat country as far as they could see. "Some people think that it is a boundary of giants," Leowulf said with a shrug.

But, when the others had ridden out of earshot, Leowulf warned Olaf: "You must beware of that knave Godrich."

"Who is Godrich, Lord?" Olaf asked in surprise. "Is he The Bear?"

Leowulf bellowed with loud laughter. "By all the gods, that is a good jest. My Danish friend, Godrich is the Earl who calls himself King of England." Leowulf explained.

"When King Athelwald died five years ago, he left only one young daughter as his heir; and he put both her and the Kingdom under the guardianship of his wife's brother, Earl Godrich of Cornwall. King Athelwald made Godrich promise to wed his daughter to the most powerful man in the whole of England; 'for,' he said, 'when she is Queen of

England, she will need a husband who can guard her well. But Earl Godrich calls himself King and I believe that he means to stay in power despite the Lady Goldenburg's good title to the kingdom. Perhaps he will wed her to his baby son, in order to rule England in his little son's name. But he keeps our good Lady under lock and key; and I am afraid that one day he will get rid of her."

Olaf was too startled to speak; and Leowulf went on quickly, "I did not like the way Godrich looked at you, when you were talking to the Lady Goldenburg. He has some evil thoughts; and I fear that he means to make trouble for you. Watch out for a swipe of the royal staff; and duck away from it, if you can, Olaf. But, if you do find yourself in trouble, remember that I, Leowulf, am your sworn friend; for I am ready to help you at any time, I myself and all my men.

"If ever you need my help, come or send a message to my burgh at Elmham," Leowulf told Olaf. "It is only a day's ride across the Norfolk fens from Crowland Abbey; and, once you reach the fens, even the King could not catch you without my help. I am taking you to Crowland now, to show the monks that you are my sworn friend. Then, if need arises, they will help you for my sake; for I built their abbey; and I guard them against Viking robbers."

Leowulf spoke no more to Olaf during the journey; and during the evening the talk was all about strongmen and the Games. But the next morning, when the men from Lincoln had mounted to go home, Leowulf walked over to bid Olaf Godspeed; and he said quietly in Danish, "Do not forget, my friend, what I told you yesterday. Watch that fox Godrich, when you meet him again; and, if you are in danger, either come or send word to me in East Anglia."

At Lincoln Olaf lived as before the Great Games. Thane Harald taught him how to handle the sword and the shield, the axe and the staff, the ten-foot-long stabbing spear and the short throwing spear; and Master Eric taught him the arts of wrestling and putting the weight. Meanwhile, Olaf worked in the kitchen and armoury of Lincoln Castle and earned his keep.

Olaf began to think that he was now strong enough to throw the stone further than Thorard Blackbeard and to outwrestle him. He made up his mind to go to Grimsby soon; for he needed Grim's help to return to Denmark and to wreak his revenge. But one day in September, after a long bout of weapon training, Thane Harald suddenly said: "Tomorrow, Olaf, you must help the carpenters to build two bowers beside the hall. For the Lord King is coming to Lincoln next week; and he will live in the Castle, while the Witan meets."

"What is the Witan, Lord?"

"The Witan— or the Witenagemot as it should be called— is the Great Council of the English people. The King has summoned all his thanes and the Earls, Bishops and Abbots of England to give him counsel at Michaelmas."

The King's Reeve studied his leather boot and reasoned aloud:

"The Witan has met only once since the death of King Athelwald. At that meeting Earl Godrich was given the title of 'King'; for King Athelwald's heir, the Lady Goldenburg, was not yet old enough to be wed and to be Queen. But the Lady Goldenburg is now fourteen years old and so fully of age to be wed."

The Reeve paused. Then he added thoughtfully: "The Lord King is bringing the Lady to Lincoln. So perhaps he has called the Witan to choose her husband and to give her the Kingdom which is her birthright. But I wonder . . .'he mused, and stared at his boot.

"Don't fret about that, Olaf," said the Reeve. "But I have it in my mind to ask the Lord King to give you a place in his household. So do not quarrel with any of his men."

Olaf had not forgotten Leowulf's warning; and the news of the King's coming made him want to run away to Grimsby at once. But the news that the Lady Goldenburg was also coming and the memory of her whispered words encouraged him to stay. He was eager to go back to Denmark to beat his Uncle Thorard; but even more he wanted to see the Lady again. Therefore, he waited impatiently for Michaelmas.

On Michaelmas Eve the King and his household rode up through the town and into the Castle. First came the King's grooms and kennelmen, leading the King's horses and hunting hounds. Next came a long train of pack-horses and carts. The pack-horses carried the King's bed, his seat and many carved chests; but the carts carried larger, rougher chests, which held the King's cups, bowls and dishes and his cook's pots and pans; and beneath each cart a watch-dog was tied. Then came the courtiers in brightly coloured clothes and the priests in black; and after them rode the Lady Goldenburg among the King's women; but the rightful Queen was so tightly wrapped and so closely guarded that few people could see her. Last of all came the King, armed himself and guarded by three hundred mail-clad men with spears and axes ready.

When the King dismounted, he asked Thane Harald: "Is that fisherman's brat, the kitchen-boy strongman, still here?"

"He is here, Lord King." the Thane answered, "but I hope that you will take him into your own household; for he would be a good man for your guard."

The King looked surprised. "My own household?" he asked, then chuckled. "Perhaps! Perhaps!" he said; and he turned away with an amused smile.

After supper the King grew bored with the clowns and jugglers who were amusing the crowd in the large hall; and he sent one of his men to bring Olaf to his bower. "Olaf Strongman!" said the King, when the kitchen-boy knelt before him. "It is high time that you were wed."

Olaf looked up in amazement. "But, Lord King, I have neither land nor silver. I can hardly find food and clothing for myself alone. How could I keep a wife?"

With his hand the King brushed Olaf's words aside. "You are strong," he said. "And I will help you to make a good living. You can be a spearman in my household; and, if you please me, I may make you a thane."

The King paused and added slowly: "Also, the wife whom I have chosen for you brings a dowry of thirty silver shillings."

The King held up a heavy leather purse and clanked the silver in it. But Olaf still fidgeted. "Lord King, I did not mean to take a wife yet" he muttered stubbornly.

The King's red face flushed redder still; and he shouted angrily: "Stop blathering like a sheep, boy. Take this purse; and go and make ready your best clothes. For at sun-up tomorrow you shall be wed."

Olaf ran to the kitchen and told Master Eric the amazing news. The steward cried out with surprise; but he said proudly: "I remember when you fought the beggars on Wigford Wharf. Who would have guessed then that the King himself would give you a bride and thirty shillings as well?"

"But I don't want a wife," Olaf complained. "And, if the King is forced to sweeten her with silver, she must be as sour as an unripe apple."

"Whatever she looks like, boy, you must take her and thank the King for his kindness," the steward advised. "If her face is ugly, just keep your mind on the shining silver. That will make you smile."

Master Eric's wife pressed the good woollen clothes which Olaf had worn to the Mayday Games. Then she trimmed his hair, so that it fell evenly to his shoulders all round; and she brushed it, till it shone like gold; and, while she brushed, she chattered:

"Whoever the bride is, she should be very happy to wed such a handsome man as you are, Olaf. And you won't need to work in the kitchen any more. The King will find you a place in his household; and perhaps one day he might make you steward of one of his halls. But I wonder whom the King has chosen for your wife."

Early the next morning Thane Harald came to see that his kitchen-boy was ready for his wedding; and he gave him a silver brooch, to fasten his mantle at the shoulder. Then he stood back and inspected the young bridegroom. "There is a man whom ANY woman should be pleased to wed. Eh, Master Eric?" the Thane said proudly

"Truly, Lord, he makes a handsome bridegroom. But who is the bride?" asked the steward.

Olaf looked hopefully at the Thane; but the old warrior shook his head. "I do not know the bride" he said. "But I believe that the King has chosen one of the women of his own household; for there has been a stir in his women's bower this morning."

Then the Thane told Olaf: "When you are called into the hall, remember to take your mantle from your shoulders. . Kneel before the King; and bow to any others who seem from their clothes to be lords or churchmen. Then walk over to me; and stand still, until you are told what to do. Whatever the King says, do not gainsay him," the Thane warned sternly. "Just bend the knee, bow your head and thank him humbly. He was angry last night, after he had been talking to the Lady Goldenburg; for I think that she did not want to give you one of her serving maids. So let us pray God that he is not angered today. Or we may all of us feel his strength."

Thane Harald hurried away to serve his royal master; and soon Olaf was called. Master Eric shook his hand, thumped him on the shoulder and gave him good advice. "You will not find a wife so easy to master as Earl Leowulf," he said. "So pray to the gods of the heathen Danes as well as to the One True God and His Only Son; and ask them one and all to guard your ears and to strengthen your arm for clouting her."

When Olaf entered the hall, he knelt to the King, who was sitting on his seat near the fire; and then he knelt to the Lady Goldenburg, who was standing with four of her ladies. The King smiled and held out his hand. But the Lady looked away angrily; and Olaf saw that her face was swollen, as though she had been weeping.

With bowed head Olaf took his place beside Thane Harald and shyly peeped out of the corner of his eye at the four waiting-women. They were all well-born and richly dressed; but they were also, Olaf thought, rather old and hard-faced. He wondered which of them was to be his wife; and he wished very much that he had run away to Grimsby while he had the chance.

"Let us begin." the King told his chaplain.

"Very well, Lord King. Which are the couple whom you wish me to join in holy wedlock?" the priest asked.

The King beckoned to Olaf. "Stand forth, Olaf, the strongest man in England." he said with a smile; and at a push from the Thane Olaf took a pace forward and hung his head.

Then the King looked over the four waiting-women. But suddenly he pointed at the Lady Goldenburg. "Stand forth, Goldenburg," he commanded in a thunderous voice, "to be wed according to your father's will."

Olaf heard Thane Harald suck in his breath in a shocked hiss.

"But, Lord Godrich!" cried the Lady Goldenburg; and the look on her face was one of sheer horror and deep disgust.

"Don't 'Godrich' me, girl. Speak to me as your King; or hold your tongue," the King shouted harshly.

The Lady fell, weeping, on her knees before him. "Lord King!" she pleaded. "My father wanted me to wed a mighty warrior of noble blood and wide lands; for I need a husband who can guard and guide me when I become Queen." Then she pointed at Olaf; and her tearful voice became an angry wail. "But THIS man is a low-born fisherman's son."

"Your father said nothing about noble blood or wide lands, girl." King Godrich said firmly. "He told me to wed you to 'the STRONGEST man in England;' and you should be happy that God has found you such a young and handsome King of the Strongmen. If the Games at Stamford had ended otherwise, you might have had to wed that hairy Brampton Bear." he reminded her. "However, God in Heaven has chosen Strongman Olaf to be your husband."

The King rolled his eyes heavenwards and crossed himself piously; but the Lady Goldenburg jumped up and stamped her foot. "I will NOT wed a low-born kitchen-boy." she screamed at the King.

"If you disobey your King, little wench, you will be hanged in the marketplace or burned on the green," the King shouted. "So think carefully before you say no!"

Then Olaf humbly dropped upon his knee. "Lord King!" he said. "I am not a worthy husband for this great lady, who is to be Queen of England. For I am only a fisherman and a kitchen-boy"

"Stand up and take her." the King commanded Olaf. "She is young and fair. She can keep house and salt the winter's meat, sew and do fine needlework. She will make a good wife, never fear, even if she is now a little shy. So do not make her angry by seeming unwilling to have her for your wife. Remember, too, the silver which I gave you and the thanedom of which I spoke last night," he said with a wink. "Remember also," he added harshly, "the gallows which awaits those who displease me."

In fear and trembling the little princess and the foundling kitchen-boy bowed their heads and locked their lips; and against their will they were hurriedly made man and wife forever. Then the King laughed and slapped his thighs with triumph and strode off, grinning, to the nearby church for the Witenagemot. But the Lady Goldenburg fled away to her bower in angry tears; and Olaf humbly followed her.

The high-born lady chased her women out and turned on Olaf. Her grey-green eyes were as dark as the sea on a stormy winter evening; and she grabbed a distaff, with which to beat him. "I'll NEVER share my table with a sooty-handed serf. I'll NEVER let your sweaty head lie snoring on my pillow," she shouted, as she thrashed him. "Godrich's paid boy! Traitor's hireling! Judas!" she screamed with every blow, till Olaf, stung to anger, seized the distaff.

"Lady, I knew nothing about the King's plan to have us wed. I was forced as much as you," he said.

As they struggled, wisps of wool flew off the cleft stick onto her nose and mouth; and she let go the distaff, to wipe her itching face. "Beast! Ruffian! Brute! Bully!" she spluttered and pommelled his chest with her fists.

"You should not call ME names." Olaf said and clasped her close against him. Suddenly she could neither move her arms nor even breathe; and her anger turned to helpless tears.

"No!" she agreed. "It is my father's false friend Godrich who is the Judas. It is that sly Cornish Fox who is the traitor.

"But how shall I get the Kingdom which is mine, now that I am wedded to a low-born churl's son?" she wailed. "Who will remember that my father was King, when I am a nobody's wife? Who will dare defend my lands and my gold against the greedy Godrich? Who will dare to say that I am Lady of Wessex and Queen of England in the face of Godrich's strength?"

"Lady, I am sorry for you. But do not lose hope. Remember how your eyes set me alight during the Mayday Games. Then, with the gods' help, I threw the weight further than men had believed possible. Strengthen me now with your love; and, if all the gods bless me, perhaps I may yet make you Queen of England."

The great lady saw little hope of help from a kitchen-boy; but Olaf patted her shoulder and stroked her hair with kindly gentleness; and after a while she laid her head against his chest and dried her tears on his tunic.

Then he advised her firmly: "Lady, I think that we should leave Lincoln at once, while King Godrich is busy in the church. If we stay here, we shall be in his hands; and I am afraid that he may hurt you or shame you further. By my advice, Lady, we should flee to the fens. We can go to East Anglia, where my sworn friend Earl Leowulf is master; or we can go to Grimsby, where my foster-father Grim is the headman. I have heard that Earl Leowulf is here for the Witenagemot; and it would be unwise to put the

King against him now, when he is in the King's city. Later we may need Earl Leowulf's help; but now I should like to go back to Grimsby; for the Danish fishermen among whom I grew up will guard us well."

"You are right, Olaf. We ought to leave Lincoln as soon as we can. Take me wherever you think best," the Lady said meekly.

The Lady Goldenburg covered her rich clothes with a coarse woollen travelling cape and cowl; and she tied her jewels in a little leather bag. Neither Olaf nor his bride told anyone that they were leaving; and they did not even take horses from the stable. They left the Castle by a small door, which was used only by servants and slaves; and they soon mingled with the crowd outside. Then they left the town among the country people and walked over the Wolds towards Grimsby.

Olaf thought that they had got away unseen; but Godrich's spies had watched them go and said not a word to stop them. For the children had done just what Godrich wanted them to do. With Goldenburg safely out of the way, he could tell the Witan any tale that he liked.

CHAPTER VIII

THE WEDDING FEAST

Goldenburg was used to travelling on horseback; and the long walk over the hills tired her. By the time that they came in sight of Grimsby, the sun was far down in the western sky; and Olaf had been carrying his bride for many miles. Both had enjoyed it; for Goldenburg felt safe and comfortable in Olaf's strong arms; and Olaf began to believe that the great lady truly was his wife.

Three years earlier, when Olaf left Grimsby, the Danish fishermen had had lean fishing and empty bellies. Now, as he looked at the village before him, signs of wealth greeted his eyes. There were new boats and new houses. Strong nets were drying on the poles; good woollen clothes were airing on the bushes; and the children playing around the huts were fat and rosy.

"Ho there!" Olaf called to a lanky girl, who was gathering some of the clothes which had dried in the sun. "Where can I find Master Grim?"

The girl's eyes opened as round as cartwheels. She did not answer Olaf but ran into the village, shouting shrilly: "It's the Lord Olaf. If s the Lord Olaf. The Lord Olaf has come back to us."

Fishermen and their wives looked up from their nets and ran from their huts. They threw aside their headgear and cloaks and fell on their knees before the King-born. Olaf put Goldenburg down beside him and held out his hands to all his old friends. He clasped to his chest Grim's two younger sons, who had come with him from Denmark thirteen years before. "Where is Master Grim, my foster-father? And where is my eldest brother, Knut?" he asked.

"Alas, Lord Olaf! Our father died last year. After you left us, he pined away; for he felt lonely without you." Grim's sons explained.

"And where is Knut?"

"He's out fishing, Lord; but we have signalled, to recall the boats. Knut and the rest will soon be here, to share our happiness at your return"

"I see that, since I left, you have done well; for now there are many more houses and boats than there used to be; and I see many new faces."

"Yes, Lord! We have had good fishing these last two years; and many Danes have come to Grimsby, fleeing the harsh rule of false King Thorard."

"I too have done well" Olaf said proudly. "For my bride is the fairest lady in England. We were wedded only this morning; and I have brought her straight to my own people."

Then Olaf lifted the travelling cape over his bride's head; and the fisherfolk gasped, when they saw her soft white skin and rich clothes. The women and children crawled on their knees, to press Goldenburg's hand to their foreheads; and they fingered the stiff gold cloth of her tunic. The children stroked the ermine borders of her crimson velvet mantle and held the soft fur against their cheeks. But the women counted the three fine saffron-washed linen kirtles which showed below her blue silk gown; and "Oooh!" they said and "Aah!" For they never wore more than one kirtle— linen in summer and woollen stuff in winter. The fisherfolk of Grimsby had never dreamed of such luxury as this.

"She is as fair as a daughter of the gods; and she is a fit mate for Olaf, whose blood is that of kings and gods," they murmured approvingly.

An oak chest was brought to the village green; and Olaf and his bride were seated on it, to wait till Knut came; for it was the custom that the headman himself must welcome all guests and lead them to his hall.

Meanwhile the villagers stared in wonder at the handsome King-born and his lovely wife.

Goldenburg was amazed to see how the villagers humbled themselves in the presence of her low-born husband. They bared their heads and threw off their cloaks, when they came near. They bent the knee before him; they kissed the hem of his tunic; and they placed his hand upon their foreheads. They even laid their heads and hands upon his knees, as though they were doing homage to their master.

The Danes called Olaf 'Lord' and 'King;' but Goldenburg could not understand what they said; for she spoke only Anglo-Saxon and a little Norman-French and Latin. Olaf knew that his bride was puzzled but afraid to question him in public. He hoped that he could keep her in doubt until they were alone; and, when he thought how surprised she would be when she learnt the truth about him, his eyes shone.

"His fiery soul is blazing in his eyes," cried one of Grim's grandchildren. With a laugh Olaf jumped up, threw the little boy high into the air and caught him. But the boy shrieked with fear; and Olaf quickly put him down again beside his mother. "Have you then forgotten how we used to play, little Olaf Knutson?" he asked shyly.

The Danes, kneeling in a circle round Olaf and Goldenburg, nudged one another and laughed happily at their kindly lord; and Olaf felt Goldenburg's small, soft hand creep into his own. She felt at ease among these friendly people.

Then Olaf saw Knut, his eldest foster-brother, running from his boat; and, taking Goldenburg's hand, he ran to meet him. There was laughter and tears and love and respect in their greeting; and Knut shouted eagerly to the villagers: "Men! Bring up two ships; and spread sails between them for a roof. Women! Spice your best mead and bake your best bread. For tonight we feast in joy and thanks because the Lord Olaf has brought his fair bride to us."

But for Olaf himself Knut had weightier words. "When our father died, Lord, the last words that he spoke were: 'See that Olaf King-born wants for nothing. We are his men, to do him service; and all our goods are his, to use as he wishes; and all our lives are his, to win him back his land.'

"Grim left us, his sons, beasts by the score and many good fishing-boats. But to YOU he left a chest full of gold and silver and three twentfour-oar ships, with war-shirts and helmets, shields and sharp weapons enough for three ships' crews. 'When the

King goes home,' the old man used to say, 'he will need ships and well-armed men about him. "

Olaf listened with tears in his eyes; for even in the grave Grim was his faithful guardian and helper; and Grim's three sons were as loyal to him as their father had been.

"Live with us, Lord" the Grimsons begged him; "and we will build you the best hall in Lindsey. You shall be our headman and your wife our lady. We will give you everything you need. Our wives and daughters will cook your meals and wash your clothes and clean your house and make your bed; and our sons will carry water for your wash-basin and rushes for your floor and wood for your fire. We could not allow our lord and his wife to do such things; for your wife must live like a great lady; and our daughters will be her serving maids, to undress her at night and dress her in the morning."

"Perhaps!" said Olaf, putting his arms around his brothers' shoulders. "At the very least my wife and I will spend our wedding night here; and tomorrow we will talk about the future. But, whether we go or stay, we shall be forever thankful for your love."

In the last sunlight the fishermen stretched chequered sails and canvas boat-covers, to roof the space between two beached ships; the women cooked;

and the children ran excitedly about, carrying things and dropping things and getting in the way. But Olaf and Goldenburg rested their weary legs in Knut's hall. Suddenly they heard the thundering hoofs of horses in the village; and a frightened child came running, to tell the headman: "Lord! Lord! A large gang of Englishmen is asking for 'Strongman Olaf' Their leader is dark-skinned, black-haired and as big as a troll."

"I know who THAT is." Olaf cried; and he ran out into the twilight, to greet Earl Leowulf.

"My friend!" said Leowulf. "King Godrich, with tears in his eyes, told the Witan that the Lady Goldenburg, his ward, had run off with a churl's son; He said that against his wishes she had thrown away the Kingdom of England for the light love of a handsome knave. I thought that Godrich's 'handsome knave' might be you, strongman; and I have come to see if you need any help."

"King Godrich lied," Olaf said angrily. "Early this morning he called us to his seat; and he threatened the Lady Goldenburg with a shameful death unless she obeyed him. He said that her father had told him to wed her to 'the strongest man in England;' and against her will he wedded her to ME. Earl Godrich may hope that the English will not have a kitchen-boy for King; and he may hope to steal not only her kingdom but also her lands and goods."

"Godrich was partly right," Leowulf said grimly. "The Witan deemed and doomed that a churl's son could not be King; and they chose to make Godrich King of England. But they also deemed that the Lady Goldenburg is rightfully Lady of Wessex; and they deemed that all her father's belongings now rightly belong to her. Godrich was very angry," Leowulf said with a grin.

"Come and tell your news to the Lady Goldenburg," Olaf urged. But Leowulf took his arm.

"Wait, Strongman Olaf. During the Mayday Games I saw a black mark on your shoulder. What is it?"

Olaf looked at the ground. "Perhaps it was mud," he muttered.

"No! It was neither mud nor a freckle nor any churl's birthmark," Leowulf said firmly. "It was a raven's head; and by chance I have seen that mark once before. When I was a boy, my uncle took me to the Games; and on that day I saw another strongman who had this same mark on his shoulder. He was Mighty Magnus, the King of the Danes; and, if only you had a big yellow beard, you would look just like King Magnus.

"It is indeed strange that you should talk about the King of the Danes," Olaf said lightly. "For I have it in my mind to go and see how he fares in his own land."

"But King Magnus has been dead for many years," said Leowulf in surprise. "He died of his wounds after a great sea battle."

"But that knave Thorard is not dead yet," Olaf muttered savagely under his breath; and he clenched his hands, as though they held Thorard's windpipe.

Leowulf saw Olaf's scowl and knotted fingers; and he shrugged crossly; for he wanted to help his young friend. But soon he grinned and thumped him on the back. "I see, Strongman, that you want to hide your birth and blood. But, whether you are churl's son or king's son, never forget that I am your sworn friend; and remember that I will give you all the help that I can whenever you ask for it."

"I thank you and love you for your kindness, Lord." Olaf said; and he clasped Leowulf's hand. "The Lady Goldenburg and I do not need your help now; for we have some business over the sea. But, if we do well beyond the sea, we shall come back to England; and then we may need your help. Come now; and tell the Lady Goldenburg your news about the Witan.

Afterwards bring your men to join the wedding feast which my friends, the fisherfolk of Grimsby, are giving for me tonight."

"Will so many Englishmen be welcome in a Danish village?" Leowulf asked doubtfully. "If so, we have brought wine and meat enough for a king's hall."

"Since you are my friends, you would be welcome, even if you were trolls; and, since you also can speak Danish, these kind people will love you as I do," Olaf answered firmly.

"Now come and meet the Lady Goldenburg and the village headman, who is my foster-brother. But if the Lady asks questions about me, Lord," he added urgently, "you must say nothing about the raven's head. If it is there, she can find it for herself."

The Lady Goldenburg and Knut welcomed Leowulf and his men; and the villagers gladly took the wine and meat which they had brought. Leowulf told the Lady his news about the Witan; but, when she asked him why the Danish villagers behaved so humbly towards her kitchen-boy husband, he answered: "Lady, it is a wonder to me, as it is to you. But perhaps in Denmark Olaf was not a churl's son; and perhaps in the past these humble folk were his father's men"

"Lord Leowulf, I wish to know the truth about the man to whom I was wedded by force; but I cannot speak Danish. Ask the headman why they all kneel to Olaf as though he was a god." she commanded.

"Lady, it is not right that you should ask me to do that." Leowulf answered sternly. "To speak plainly, Lady, you should ask Olaf; and, when he is ready, he will tell you what you want to know. One thing I can tell you," he added earnestly. "No woman ever had a man of stronger body or stouter heart than YOUR husband."

Goldenburg was angry, because Leowulf had scolded her; but already she felt proud to hear her husband praised by so great a man. So she said nothing; and Leowulf took her hand and humbly pressed it to his forehead.

"By God's will, Lady," he said from his heart, "you may yet become Queen of England and my sworn Lord. If so, I want no other King by your side than Olaf the Strong."

Soon they were led to the feast laid out between two tarred ships and below an awning of sails. The place of honour was given to the King-born kitchen-boy; and on one side of him sat his royal bride, the Lady Goldenburg; and on his other side sat his sworn friend, Earl Leowulf. They ate, drank, sang songs and listened to tales for many hours; but the best tale of all was told by Earl Leowulf.

When Leowulf arose among the empty tables and gazed around the shining faces, the Minstrel-God took hold of him. Leowulf loomed huge and unearthly in the flickering light of the smouldering fire and flaming pine torches. His eyes stared, wild as a berserk's; sweat dripped from his beard; and the proud words rolled from his deep chest like the music of drums. Leowulf told the fishermen a story which they had not yet heard. He told them 'Olaf's Saga' the story of the Great Summer Games at Stamford.

First Leowulf told how Olaf threw the stone like a god; then he told of Olaf's staff play with the "Bear;" and last he told of the three long bouts of wrestling between Olaf and himself. He told it so well that all who heard him felt each grip and heave; and they shuffled their shoes in the dust with each shift of the wrestlers feet. The listeners' hands grasped the air; and their legs strained against an unseen enemy. Sweat ran down their faces; and groans and grunts were wrung from their writhing bodies.

Although the fishermen were sitting safely by their own fireside, each of them fought hard for Olaf, their dear Lord; and, when the tale ended, many wondered whether they had in truth been listening to Leowulf.

Some thought that "Olaf's Saga" had been told by Odin, chief of the Danish gods; for in Valhalla, the heavenly home for Danish heroes, it was Odin who told the warriors' tales of fame.

Whether it was Leowulf or Odin himself who had sung Olaf's praises, the feasters were bound with a strong spell. For a long moment after the minstrel fell silent, the listeners sat still and dumb with wonder. Then their cheering smashed the silence; and after the roar of thunderous applause came golden lightning and a silver shower; for rings and brooches rained on Leowulf, as the Minstrel-God went out of him and he sat down, dazed and empty.

CHAPTER IX

RETURN TO DENMARK

When the torches had burned low and many of the feasters slept where they sat, the women led Goldenburg away.

"Where are you going?" Olaf asked. But the women only giggled; and the men guffawed.

At last Knut whispered: "They are taking the bride to be undressed and put into the wedding-bed." And Olaf blushed for his foolish question.

At a sign from the women, Knut, Leowulf and the men grabbed hold of Olaf; and, roaring the wedding-song, they carried him high on their shoulders to the bower at the end of Knut's hall. There on the pillow Olaf saw the scared face of his bride. He smiled at her, to give her comfort; but soon he was too shy to look at her; for his friends were stripping him of all his clothes.

Soon Olaf was as naked as the day that he was born. Laughing and joking, his friends lifted the blanket and thrust him into bed beside his bare bride.

The bride and bridegroom lay together side-by-side; but they stayed as still and straight as two logs, because they were bashful. All the jests and gibes of the wedding guests could not make them kiss.

When their noisy friends had gone and shut the door, Goldenburg turned her head upon the pillow; and she blurted out the question which all evening she had wanted to ask. "I wish to know," she demanded regally, "why these Danish fishermen behave so humbly to us. At first I thought that they knelt to you because you had wedded a king's daughter; but now I think that they kneel to me because I am YOUR wife. Olaf, why do the Danes treat you like a god?" she asked sternly.

"Fair lady, your eyes are brighter than stars; and your skin is softer and sweeter than rose petals." he said to please her. And then he replied to her question: "Although you do not know the Danish tongue, you have already glimpsed the truth. These simple Danes live far from English towns and pass their days on the sea. They do not know you as rightful Queen of England. From your rich clothes they understand that you are a lady of high birth; and they say that you are as fair as a daughter of the

Danish gods. But me they love very much, because I was brought up with them since childhood; and they kneel to me, because in the Danes' land I was not a churl's son."

"But, Olaf, who WAS your father?" Goldenburg pressed him.

"Ask me no more questions tonight, good wife. I am very sleepy after such a busy day. Come! Blow out the lamp; and let us go to sleep." Olaf spoke gruffly; but, as he turned his back on his puzzled bride and pretended to be asleep, he smiled to himself. He heard her blow out the lamp; and in the darkness he felt her toss and turn. For Goldenburg was tormented by doubts; and her deep-seated pride in her royal blood was at war with her growing fondness for her low-born husband.

But Olaf himself soon fell asleep; and, as he slept, he dreamed a dream, so that he also flung the bedclothes about. Suddenly he was awakened by soft hands on his arms; and he felt a soft cheek on his cheek and soft lips on his lips. Then, as he swam up from the deeps of sleep, he clasped his warm bride to his chest; and he whispered wonderingly: "I dreamt that I stood on a hill and looked over all the land of the Danes. I brushed my hands across the moors of Denmark. The Earls' strong camps crumbled at my touch; and all the people clung to my arms. Then the Danes climbed upon my back; and I flew over the sea; and I clasped England tightly to my breast. But now I find that England is you, my wife, my queen."

"Oh, Olaf!" Goldenburg whispered: "While you slept, I was bewailing my lost kingdom, hating Godrich for his treachery and scorning you for being low-born. But, when I remembered your loving kindness, my hard hate was melted and my cold scorn warmed; and I looked at you in the half-light.

"Then I saw a wonder, dear husband. The light in the bower came from your face and shone from your mouth. By the light of your own bright breath, I saw your meekness and your boldness, your unscarred beauty and your supple strength; and I loved you, Olaf. I stroked your arms, with their iron sinews clothed in silken skin; and on your shoulder I found a little mark like a black raven's head. Then I knew the truth, My Lord. Then I knew why the Danes kneel before you and bow their heads upon your knees. Then I knew that you are their true-born King"

"A King without a Kingdom wedded to a Queen without a Realm!" laughed Olaf.

"But that is the meaning of your dream, My Lord." cried Goldenburg. "Soon you will hold the land of Denmark in your hands; and soon you will clasp the land of England against your breast. But talk of that tomorrow. Tonight, dear husband, be content with ME. Hold ME in your hands, dear heart; and clasp ME against your breast; but treat me gently, my King of the Strongmen."

The next morning Leowulf and his men took leave of the Lady Goldenburg with the honour due to a princess; and they took leave of Olaf with the love due to a sworn friend.

"May God keep you safe, until we meet again, golden man," Leowulf said. "I shall spread the story of how the fox forced the goldfinch to wed a sparrow. Yes! I shall tell the tale with cunning; and, when England learns that the sparrow was a royal raven, the sly fox will be laughed to scorn."

But Olaf just smiled and shook his head, as though he did not understand. "You talk in riddles, Lord Leowulf; and my brain does not match my brawn," he said lightly. "But, when I return from my voyage to Denmark, I shall visit you; and I may then ask your help to get back my wife's belongings. Meanwhile, I beg you, do not talk of ravens."

Leowulf and his bodyguard rode away down the coast and took ship across the Wash to East Anglia. But Olaf and his bride rode to a monastery, to confess their sins; and they sought a blessing on their voyage to Denmark.

When Olaf asked the three Grimsons to come with him across the sea, they fell on their knees. "Lord, this is the day for which we have waited" they cried eagerly, "when our King goes back to claim his Kingdom. As we fled from Denmark with our King, so will we go back with our King; for we must wreak revenge upon that traitor Thorard."

Every Dane in Grimsby offered his services; but Olaf wanted to take only one twelve-bench ship. He hoped to find out whether the Danes in Denmark would support King Magnus' son against the usurper Thorard; for he needed to know that, before he risked everything in a war. For that reason he chose only seventy two young men to pull the twenty-four oars in three shifts; and he swore the people of Grimsby to secrecy. Strong war-shirts, helmets and shields, as well as sharp spears, swords and axes from old Grim's store were given to Olaf's crew. But he himself dressed like a merchant in a wide-brimmed hat and long cloak; and he loaded a cargo of trade goods.

When the ship was ready to sail, Olaf took Goldenburg in his arms. "Wife!" he said, "My voyage will be rough, cold and wet. And, even though I am rightfully their King, the Danes may kill me, when I get there. If you come with me, you will be far from your homeland and in great discomfort; and you may even lose your life. But, if you stay here, these kind Grimsby people will guard and serve you as their Queen. What will you do?"

"Loving Lord and lordly lover, I shall come with you," Goldenburg answered with a steady voice. "I have no home but in your arms, no safety but under your hand, no comfort but beside your warm body. Your victory shall be my delight; or, if God wills it, we will die together."

Olaf just held her tightly and looked at her; for his heart lumped so large in his throat that he could not speak.

After listening to the latest news from Denmark, Olaf decided to land at Tonning near the mouth of the River Eider; for the town of Tonning was near the camp of a very powerful Danish earl called Ubbe. Olaf remembered that Earl Ubbe had been his father's sword-friend and had saved his own life at the ship-funeral. Furthermore, Ubbe was said to be a good Christian; and it was well known that he greatly disliked the false King Thorard. For all these reasons Olaf hoped to get advice and help from Ubbe.

The voyage to Denmark was quick and smooth; for the wind was westerly; and the winter storms had not yet begun. Olaf anchored his ship in the haven below the wooden walls of Tonning. Then he was rowed ashore and walked up to Earl Ubbe's camp.

When Olaf was led into the Earl's long hall, Ubbe was seated on the dais at the far end. The old warrior was thick-set and upright, as hard and tough as the oak chest on which he sat. He was wearing a coat of black boiled leather and baggy trousers of hairy yellow cloth; and his trousers were cross-gartered from ankle to knee with broad leather straps. With his right hand he held a short, heavy, iron-bladed boar-spear; and with his left hand he fondled the ears of a huge, shaggy hound, which lay across his feet, forever on guard.

Ubbe watched the big, golden-haired youth walking up the hall towards him. He wondered whose man Olaf was and the reason for his visit. When Olaf bent the knee and held out a Saxon ring, Ubbe did not take it; for he was wise and very wary of strangers. "What do you want?" he asked bluntly.

"Lord, I bring this ring, which is a gift to your wife from mine." answered Olaf, honey-tongued.

"What else do you want?" asked the Earl; for he could see that the ring was gold; and strangers do not give gold for nothing.

"Lord, I am a trader," Olaf said. "I ask leave to pass up the River Eider to the trading town Hedeby on the Baltic Sea."

The Earl doubted that Olaf was truly a trader; and he spoke the thought which was uppermost in his mind. "It seems to me that such a mighty man as you ought rather to be a warrior bearing arms; for traders fight only in the marketplace; and instead of swords they wield windy words. Your strong body is utterly wasted in trade."

Olaf said nothing; and for a while the two men stared silently at each other. Then suddenly the Earl leant forward and took the ring from Olaf's hand. "I like you" he said; "and I shall not pry into your business. You may cross my land to Hedeby, as you ask"

Olaf bowed low with muttered thanks and started to leave. But the Earl thumped the dais with his spear-butt; and the hound growled. Olaf wondered what he had done wrong; and he stood quite still.

"A small twelve-bench ship with three shifts of oarsmen is no place for a woman." Earl Ubbe said.

"Your wife ought to sleep ashore, trader. Bring her to take supper at my table tonight."

Olaf was taken aback by this command; for he had not known that Ubbe was so well informed; and he did not want to bring Goldenburg into danger. He shuffled his feet before the bleak stare of the Earl's blue eyes. "Lord, my wife is too shy to come ashore; for she is a Saxon; and she can speak no Danish at all" he said feebly.

"My wife and I both speak Saxon," the Earl assured him. "We shall make your wife feel at home here, trader."

The Earl's face was stern; but Olaf spoke again. "Also, Lord, I am afraid of your men; for Danish warriors sometimes kill a man just to take his wife."

"Trader, that may happen in other men's halls; but it will not happen here." the old Earl snapped. Then he added loudly, so that all in his hall could hear the warning: "If any man harms either you or your wife while you are my guests, he shall HANG. You have my word on THAT."

Earl Ubbe thumped the dais with the butt of his spear and pointed with his chin towards the door. Then he turned away, to spit on the floor; the hound went to sleep; and Olaf bowed himself out of the great man's hall and went back to his ship.

112

That evening Olaf wrapped Goldenburg in a travelling-cape and hid her face in its cowl. He carried her in his arms like a sleeping child; and as armed guard he took two of Grim's sons. When they reached Earl Ubbe's hall, they were warmly welcomed by the Earl and his wife; but the old man whispered to Olaf:

"I have never seen a Saxon woman so fair as your wife, trader Olaf. Now I understand why you were afraid to show her in a strange town. We must guard you with care; or there will be trouble."

The Earl made it clear that he thought highly of his guests; for he shared his mess of dishes with the trader's wife; and the Earl's wife shared her food with Olaf. They were served sturgeon, salmon, lampreys, venison, beef, mutton and also the meat of swans and cranes; and, to honour the guests, wine was served throughout the hall, even to the little pages sitting near the door. During the feast Olaf and Goldenburg were safe from insults and attack, because the Earl himself was with them; and afterwards the Earl sent his eldest son to take them safely to lodge with the headman of Tonning town.

When they reached the headman's house, the Earl's son shouted: "Master Sigurd!" Soon they heard the rattle of the bar being drawn; and the headman looked out. He had hastily covered his bedtime nakedness with a leather war-shirt. When he saw the Earl's son, the headman knelt humbly and touched his forehead to the great man's foot. The Earl's son said: "Master Sigurd, I greet you from my father. He bids you to give a night's lodging to this trader and his wife; for they have supped at the Earl's high table; and they will board their ship in the haven at daybreak tomorrow. The Earl bids you to guard his guests well, because they are very dear to him; and he bids you sternly not to open your door to anyone before daybreak."

Master Sigurd led Olaf and Goldenburg into his hall and barred the door. Then he cleared his sons from the sleeping-bench against the wall opposite the fire; and he told Olaf to take their place. He sent his daughters to bring more sealskins; and he sent his wife to warm and spice red wine, to give his guests a good night's sleep. However, when Olaf and Goldenburg were clad only in shirt and kirtle, there was a thunderous knocking on the door; and they heard the cry: "Open the door in Earl Ubbe's name."

"Who is there?" asked Master Sigurd.

"Open for the Earl's men," came the answer.

Master Sigurd peered out through a hole in the door. "Peaceful men do not go about the town with drawn swords in the middle of the night," he pointed out. "What do you want?"

"We want the Saxon woman," said a raucous voice amid a roar of laughter.

"Begone, drunken knaves!" Master Sigurd shouted. "I will put you in chains for breaking the night-peace of the town."

"Open the door, you peace-lover! Or we shall break it down and give you the peace of everlasting night," came the scornful answer.

"I warn you, thieves and robbers, that I have a sharp axe; and I know how to use it," Master Sigurd shouted.

Crash! The door shuddered.

Crash! The door cracked.

Crash! The door splintered.

Olaf set down his horn of wine and strolled towards the door, wiping his mouth on the back of his hand.

Then crash! A door-plank flew in; and a red face under a helmet appeared. Olaf tweaked the red nose and signed to Sigurd to be ready with his axe. Then Olaf pulled from its sockets the great oak beam which barred the double doors. The robbers dragged open the doors and rushed in.

Olaf swung the heavy beam as though it was a staff and struck three robbers across the face. They fell with smashed skulls. Again he swung the beam. Again skulls splintered. The crowd behind continued to press forward; and twenty robbers lay dead in Master Sigurd's doorway, before the rest drew back.

Then the robbers saw that Olaf was wearing nothing but his shirt. Some shot arrows at him; others threw spears or sticks or stones. Soon Olaf's shirt was ripped and bloody; and he stood, swaying, in a pool of his own blood.

Suddenly there was a cry of "Grimsby! Grimsby!" and Knut and his men came running up the road from the waterside; for the noise of battle had warned them of their lord's danger. When the robbers turned to meet the attack of the Grimsby men, Master Sigurd rushed out, whirling his axe around his head; and Olaf also staggered forward, roaring with rage and ignoring wounds or danger.

Olaf swung the door-beam from side to side like a gigantic scythe; and he smashed skulls like eggshells and snapped bones like sticks, until every enemy lay still. Bodies lay sprawled on the road and piled in the ditches. *They look like sacks of corn spilled from an overturned cart,* Olaf thought dizzily. Then he fell full-length among his enemies.

When dawn's clear light had brushed the shadows from the streets, the men of Tonning crept fearfully out of doors; and they found sixty of the Earl's men dead around the headman's house. When news of the slaughter reached Earl Ubbe, he called to arms his sons and all his hearthmen; and he rode into the town for vengeance.

The Earl looked at the sprawled bodies and the bloodstains outside the headman's house; and he looked at the battered doorway, which was as well stuck with arrows as a hedgehog is with quills. Then, roaring like a wounded bison, he called the headman. Master Sigurd was still bleeding from the battle; but he limped from his house and knelt humbly in the mud and blood beside the Earl's horse.

"Lord, armed robbers broke down my door in the middle of the night, to take the Saxon woman," he said. "They would have ransacked my house and slain us all, if the trader and his crew had not fought so well. Lord, the trader Olaf was wearing only his shirt; and he had no other arms except a heavy oak beam; but he himself slew twenty fully armed men, who broke into my house. Alas for that bold and mighty man!" he cried. "The faint-hearted knaves shot at him with arrows; and he is so badly wounded that he is likely to die."

The Earl checked the truth of the headman's story with other townsmen; and he himself felt the weight of the beam with which Olaf had fought. Then he pointed to the bodies of his men lying in the street; and he told his sons: "If any of those knaves still breathes, hang him from the gallows. I gave the trader my word on it."

To the headman he said: "Show me this mighty man. He was not made for trade; and, if he lives, he shall be my thane."

When the Earl had seen Olaf's wounds, he sent some of his men to fetch his wife; for she was skilled in healing. The old woman bandaged Olaf.'s wounds with wine-wet linen, to stop the bleeding; and she had him carried to the Earl's camp in a curtained horse litter.

Ubbe gave his guests a bed behind a screen in his own bower at the end of his hall; for he meant to guard them from the vengeance of the dead men's kin. But that night, long after the torches and oil-lamps had been put out, old Ubbe awoke; and he saw that there was a light behind the screen.

Only the wicked need lights at this time of night, Ubbe said to himself; and he pulled on his war-shirt, grasped his sword and slipped out of bed to have a look. He crept across the floor and cautiously peered round the screen. There was no one there except the trader and his wife, who were both sound asleep. But to his amazement the Earl saw that the light came from the trader's open mouth. "What can this mean?" he muttered uneasily. He was full of dread and held his sword ready to guard himself against either men or devils. But, as nothing happened, he woke his wife and sons to see the wonder; and, while they all watched, Olaf King-born turned in his sleep. Then they saw the birthmark on his shoulder— the black raven's head.

"Ah! Now I understand why this boy seemed so dear to me," Ubbe cried. "If he had a beard, he would be just like my old sword-brother, King Magnus. There on his shoulder is the King-mark." he pointed out. "And there in his mouth is the brightness of the gods' breath, which burns in the breasts only of true-born kings. This must be Olaf, the son of Mighty Magnus and the rightful King of all the Danes."

The old Earl bent over the sleeping King-born and kissed his hand warmly. But Olaf suddenly awoke and reached for his sword; and the Earl said gently: "King-born Olaf Magnusson, lie down in peace; and rest your wounded body. Forgive us, Lord, for waking you when we found out who you are; but we wish to do homage to our rightful King."

The Earl and his sons humbly knelt around the bed; and they laid their heads and hands in homage on Olaf's thighs, as though he was sitting on a King's high seat. They swore themselves Olaf's men for life. But soon old Ubbe drove his people from the bower, so that their King could regain his strength in sleep. "Your task, King-born, is to heal your wounds," he told Olaf. "My task is to call the Great Council of the Danish people; for I must tell the Great Men of the Danes that YOU, Olaf Magnusson, are their rightful King."

CHAPTER X

KING OF THE DANES

Six weeks later Earl Ubbe spoke to the Great Men of the Danes gathered in his hall. "Lords and Masters, I have called you here without leave from Earl Thorard, because not for thirteen years has he called us together. When last we met, Earl Thorard told us that King Magnus' son Olaf had been killed by a fisherman; and on that unlucky day we made Earl Thorard King.

"When Mighty Magnus was our King, he feasted us every year; he led us to many a hard-fought fight, in which we reaped riches with our swords; and, before taxing us, he listened to our counsel. But Thorard Blackbeard never feasts us nor leads us to the golden spoils of war; he never asks our counsel; and he taxes us so heavily that many Danes have fled to other lands."

Earl Ubbe paused awhile. Then slowly and clearly he declared: "Earl Thorard has no right to tax us. Many of you will remember, as I do, the day when

Mighty Magnus lay dying. He called the Great Men about his bed; and he told the priest to write his words so that his will should not be forgotten. The King said that his son Olaf should be King of the Danes when he was a grown man; and he made it treason for any man to harm the boy.

"Earl Thorard and we who stood around the bed swore a great oath to obey the King's words. But, Lords and Masters, Earl Thorard soon forswore his oath. With his own hand he slew the King's two daughters; and with his own hand he bound the King's heir and told a fisherman to drown the child. By luck, that fisherman saw the gods' bright breath burning in the boy's mouth; and he saw the "King-mark' on the boy's shoulder. Then he knew that the boy whom Thorard had told him to drown was the rightful King; and he took the King-born to safety in England. Now, fourteen years after King Magnus' death, his son Olaf has come to claim his Kingdom. Yes! Olaf the Strong has come to wreak revenge upon the traitor Thorard."

At those words Olaf strode from the bower onto the dais. He towered above the old warrior Ubbe; and his hair and beard lay like gold lace upon the greasy grey mail which covered his broad shoulders and deep chest. The Danes gasped at his size and beauty;

and some of the older men thought that Mighty Magnus again stood before them.

"Behold, you Danes, your King!" cried Ubbe. "The fairest and strongest man in the land, who bears his father's likeness on his face and body. The gods' breath burns so brightly in his breast that at night there is no darkness near him; and upon his shoulder is the black raven's head, the birth-mark of our Danish Kings. Behold Lord Olaf's wife, who is far fairer than the apple blossom and sweeter than the apple! The Lady Goldenburg is good King Athelwald's only child and heir to the rich Kingdom of England. Speak out, you Great Men of the Danes! Will you follow King Olaf to victory and to riches?"

Those who knew King Magnus could see that Olaf looked just like him.

Some needed no more proof of his claim to be King; and they raised their spears and shouted, "Olaf is our King."

But others looked doubtful and talked uneasily amongst themselves; and one of the doubters stepped forward and spoke to the crowded hall: "Lords and Masters! It is no light matter for the free Danes to do homage to a King. Some of us are too young to remember Mighty Magnus; and some of us need to see better proof of this man's claim to the Kingship."

123

Olaf could see that even those who earlier had acknowledged him now looked doubtful. But Ubbe's scarred and leathery face still smiled serenely. "Lords and Masters, I am not a fool," he said. "I should not do homage to a stranger, just because he looks like my old King. But the burning breath and the mark of the raven are more than likenesses. Those are the sure and sacred signs of kingship. There is still more proof of the Lord Olaf's claim. I and three others, who stood around King Magnus' bed as he lay dying, have questioned the Lord Olaf; and he has told us all that happened at the King's deathbed and also at the ship-funeral. He remembers word for word Mighty Magnus' commands; and he told us too the oaths which were sworn by Earl Thorard and all of us who were there. There is no doubt that the Lord Olaf who now stands before us is one and the same as the little King-born who saw and heard King Magnus make this will."

Earl Ubbe waved a large parchment with wax seals at its foot; and he showed it to those who stood nearest to him. It was King Magnus' will, signed with his own blood and witnessed by the seals of all the Danish Earls. Most of the men were now ready to take Olaf as their rightful King; but doubt still showed on some faces; and there was much argument.

Then Olaf saw an old man, with a sadly twisted face, standing on a chest at the far end of the hall. The old man was beating the mud wall with his spear, trying to get silence so that he could speak.

"Lords and Masters!" Ubbe shouted, "Old Scarface Gunder, who knew King Magnus well, wishes to speak to you. Will you not hear him?" The babble of argument died down; and in a slow, cracked voice the old man spoke: "Lords, I was huntsman to Mighty Magnus from his boyhood until his death. I looked after his spears, his bows and arrows, his flaying knives and his hunting sword; and I looked after his hunting horns too."

The old man showed a horn made of a big walrus rusk, with gold mountings and a Greek silk cord.

"See this horn, Lords! The good King gave it to me on the day that he died. He called me to his bed, Lords; and he said to me: 'Gunder, old friend!' he said, 'I'll not be hunting with you again, until you reach Valhalla; but I'll await you there. Now, Gunder!' he said: I want you to have my horn of walrus ivory for your own.' 'But, Lord King!' I said: 'I can't sound that horn.' 'I know,' the King said. 'There is no one who CAN sound that horn except me. But I want you

125

to keep it, friend Gunder, because, when my son grows up, HE'll be able to sound it; and he'll give you good gold for it.' "

Gunder sighed sadly. "For fourteen years," he said, "I've carried Magnus' horn; and I've been hoping to meet a man who could sound it and who would give me good gold for it. But I never yet met anyone who could sound a call on that horn, except King Magnus himself."

The old man paused, shuffled his feet and looked uneasily at Olaf. "Now, what I was thinking—" the old man began again. But his listeners could not wait for Gunder's slow thoughts and words. They shouted at him to pass the horn to Olaf. Then the old huntsman nodded his head and smiled his approval; and he handed the horn to the man nearest to him. That man tried the horn and blew his hardest; and so did every other man who handled it on its way to Olaf at the far end of the hall.

By the time that the horn had reached the dais, everybody was laughing; for no one could get from that horn any more than a squeak, a whistle or a hiss. One man blew so hard that he had a fit and had to be carried out; and several men were doubled up with laughter. But, when Ubbe himself put the horn to his lips, the crowd fell silent; for Ubbe was the most famous hunter in Denmark, a man who had hunted almost every day for fifty years. Ubbe blew the horn three times with all his might and main. He grew purple in the face; but not a whisper broke the silence. Then, laughing ruefully, he handed the horn to Olaf.

A deep silence settled on the hall. But Olaf held the horn awkwardly; and he blushed and made excuses. "Lords, I do not know how to blow a horn," he said. "Never in all my life have I blown one. I should feel foolish trying to sound a horn, when so many good hunters have failed."

A man in the crowd pointed his thumb at Olaf and shouted scornfully: "King Magnus said that his son would be able to sound the horn. So, if you ARE Olaf Magnusson, let us hear you sound a good, long note."

There was a growing murmur of scoffing words and mocking laughter in the crowded hall. Unwillingly Olaf put the horn to his mouth. Again the hall was hushed; but the sniggering crowd was tiptoeing on the edge of a landslide of laughter, waiting for Olaf to fail. Olaf filled the big barrel of his chest with air and blew as hard as he could.

The whole building shivered and shuddered, throbbed and resounded with an unearthly wail; and no man there had ever heard the like, except those who had hunted with King Magnus many years before. Throughout the hall there were startled faces; but Gunder danced for joy. "Now, who is your King, my Lords and Masters?" Ubbe asked triumphantly.

Then there was a roaring and a stamping of feet; and every man in the hall drummed on his shield with his sword or spear; and they all shouted: "Olaf Magnusson is King. Olaf is our King."

Ubbe seated Olaf on his own high seat; and he seated Goldenburg beside Olaf. Then he knelt down and laid his head and hands on Olaf's knees; and he swore to be Olaf's man. Olaf put his hands over those of the old Earl and then raised him up. Each man in turn came and did homage in the same way; and Olaf covered each man's hands with his own, as a token of protection and lordship. When homage had been done, Ubbe told his men to set the trestle-tables for a feast; and, while the tables were made ready, the merry talk grew louder; for the Danes were eager to feast with their King.

However, before the dinner could be served, angry shouting was heard outside the hall; and King Thorard Blackbeard strode in through the door, with his well-armed guard behind him. Thorard was breathless and mud-spattered from riding far and fast; but he waved his sword above his head and asked angrily:

"What is this? By Thor's hammer, why do you meet without my leave at the bidding of that old dog, Ubbe?"

Earl Ubbe drew his sword with a shriek of steel; and he walked grimly towards Thorard. But a voice of thunder sounded down the hall. "Stand back, good Earl," Olaf shouted. "It is I who must try the strength of this foul knave who falsely calls himself 'King of the Danes.' "

Thorard turned furiously towards the voice; but his red face went pale, when he thought he saw his dead brother Magnus striding towards him. Olaf's face was flushed with anger; his eyes blazed like blue flames; and, when he stood looking down at his uncle, he spoke slowly through clenched teeth:

"Thorard, before my eyes you cut the throats of my two sisters. Then you beat me and made me bury their bodies; and you put a rough shirt upon my back and called me 'churl's son'. You bound and gagged me and told Grim the fisherman to drown me; and, when Grim came to you for his promised reward, you beat him and drove him away with threats. For your foul deeds you must die. But I shall not kill you yet; for I have not forgotten my dying father's words. My

129

father said: 'Olaf shall be King, as soon as he can put the weight further than Thorard and can throw him at wrestling.' Come into the yard, oath-breaker and murderer; and there the gods will show the Danes who is the true-born King and who is a false knave."

They went into the yard and stripped to their drawers; and, when the stone weight had been brought, Olaf said to Thorard: "You call yourself King. You throw first."

Thorard was a big man; and, although he was now thirty-five years old, he was still very strong. So his throw was good. Then the round stone was handed to Olaf. But Olaf prayed aloud first to his father and then to the "White Christ."

"Mighty father among the mighty gods, speed the blood of the Danish Kings through my limbs; and kindle the soul of the old gods within my breast. Oh God of the Christians, show these men that I am their rightful King," he cried to the sky and blew upon the stone.

Olaf stood with bowed head, gathering his strength and concentrating his mind for the throw. Again he warmed the stone with the gods' breath. Then he crouched and sprang with all the skill which Eric the steward had taught him. He heaved the heavy stone with god-like power.

When Thorard saw the stone flung more than twice as far as he had thrown it, he went pale; and he would have run away, if Grim's sons had not been standing at his back to stop him.

"Ayeh!" cried the Danes. "Never was such a throw made by a mere man. This is a god indeed."

"Lord Olaf!" said Ubbe, kneeling before him: "Even your father, Mighty Magnus, never made a throw as good as that; and he was the best thrower of the weight whom I ever saw. There is no need to go on with this game. Let us have done with that oath-breaker and murderer of children."

"No, old Lord!" Olaf answered. "Let the traitor try to match that throw. Let him have three more throws; and we will watch him sweat and strain to keep his life against the gods' will."

Thorard threw again and again and yet again, with the strength of desperation; but he reached scarcely more than halfway to Strongman Olaf's mark. Then Ubbe and the Grimsons gathered round Thorard, to take their revenge. But Olaf stopped them.

"My father said that I must also be able to throw Earl Thorard at wrestling," he said. "Make a ring for us, Lords and Masters; and appoint two good men to judge the falls." "What do you say, Uncle?" Olaf asked Thorard. "Shall we wrestle the best of three falls? Or

131

shall one fall decide who is the King and who is the traitor?"

"Let us wrestle three falls, you mongrel puppy," Thorard snarled, "lest you have a lucky throw."

Then the two men wrestled, the dark-skinned Thorard and his fair-skinned, golden-haired nephew; and Olaf was bigger, stronger and more skillful. Olaf had never forgotten the brutal wrestling lesson which Thorard had given him when he was a small boy. Growling with his hatred, he threw Thorard down, pulled him up and threw him again; and he twisted his arms and bent his legs. Soon Thorard's face was grey with pain; and his trousers were dark with sweat. But at last Olaf tired of his revenge; and he flung Thorard onto the ground and fell with his whole weight upon Thorard's chest. "One fall to Olaf!" shouted the judges.

Thorard's chest heaved for air; his breath whistled in his dry throat; his long hair and beard stuck to his sweaty skin. He could hardly rise from the ground; but he staggered to his feet and hitched up his trousers. By now Olaf was keen to bring the fight to an end; and he sprang upon Thorard, to throw him again.

"Beware the knife!" Olaf heard the warning shouted by the crowd and saw a flash of steel in Thorard's right hand striking up into his ribs. He chopped down edgeways with his left hand upon Thorard's wrist. Thorard grunted in pain; for his wrist had snapped like a hare's neck. But blood was streaming down Olaf's belly. Then Olaf seized Thorard by his beard and by the girdle of his trousers. With all the strength of his rage and hatred he lifted his wicked uncle high above his head. Then he flung him down onto the earth and jumped on him again and again, until Thorard's ribs cracked and he lay still.

When Olaf's rage had drained out of him, he turned wearily away and commanded: "Bind the traitor; and do justice upon him."

Olaf's wounds from the fight at the headman's house were scarcely healed; and now he was put to bed with a new knife-wound below the heart. Meanwhile, the Great Men judged Thorard by King Magnus' deathbed law. He was skinned alive and then hanged on the common gallows; his wife and children were hunted down and sold as slaves; and his camps and ships were given to King Olaf as compensation for the wrongs which Thorard had done him.

Everyday more Danes came to do homage to their new King. The council of Great Men advised Olaf how to right the wrongs done by Thorard; and they agreed to raise three hundred ships and fifteen thousand men, to win back the Kingdom of England for Queen Goldenburg. They also undertook to become Christians; and Olaf and Ubbe stood godfather to all the councillors who were baptized.

By the time that Olaf's wounds were fully healed, the winter was nearly over; and the Danish fleet was nearly ready for the invasion of England. When the equinoctial gales had blown themselves out, Olaf made Earl Ubbe Guardian of his Kingdom; and he left Goldenburg in the care of Ubbe's wife. But he himself, with the Grimsby ship and crew, sailed secretly to England.

Olaf landed at the fishing town of Yarmouth in East Anglia. No one there knew him; and, with Knut as his only companion, he rode at once to Elmham, where Earl Leowulf had his strong burgh. Now Leowulf had heard of his sworn friend's doings in Denmark; and he was longing to tell all England how King Godrich's kitchen-boy had turned out to be the Danish King; for he was eager to make a laughing-stock of the man whom he hated. But Olaf asked him to wait a little longer; and he told him his plan for overthrowing Godrich without starting another war between the English and the Danes. Leowulf listened silently. Then he nodded in approval.

"It is a very good plan, my golden King," he said. "It is a very good plan."

"Will you help me to carry it out, Lord Leowulf?"

"I am your sworn friend, strongman King; and, even if I were not, I should help you just for the sweet joy of snaring that sly fox Godrich," Leowulf said and gave his hand upon it.

Then Olaf and Knut rode through the night back to Yarmouth; and Olaf at once set sail for Denmark. But Knut, with a heavy bag of gold, made his way to Grimsby; and there he laid in a secret store of food and gathered together as many horses as he could; and he made ready to welcome the Danish fleet.

CHAPTER XI

THE KING OF ENGLAND

K ing Godrich heard that Lady Goldenburg had become the Queen of the Danes; and he heard that a great fleet was gathering on the coast of Denmark. He guessed that, when the springtime storms were finished, the Danes would land on the east coast of England; for the east coast was the nearest to Denmark; and many Danish people already lived there. Therefore, as soon as the roads were firm enough for travel, King Godrich sent out messengers. He told the English Earls and all his own Thanes to meet him at Lincoln with all their men. He also called upon the shires and towns to send armed men according to custom; and he asked the Bishops and Abbots to bring him gold and to give him counsel.

The Great Men of England and the spearmen from many shires and towns rode and marched the muddy roads to Lincoln. Soon the monastery was full of Bishops and Abbots; many a house was hired as

136

lodging for an Earl or a great Thane; and hundreds of lesser men slept in the churches. Tents were pitched in every side-street and orchard in the town; and the grasslands between the town and the dark woods beyond were thickly freckled with tents and leafy huts.

The Great Men of England and their full war-host were gathered in Lincoln. Then one morning a muddy man galloped through the East Gate and thrust his way across the crowded marketplace. He dismounted wearily before the King's hall and gasped the dreaded news: "The Danes have landed from three hundred ships at Grimsby."

The weary messenger was dragged before the King, to tell his tale again; and at once the King sent his Thanes into every corner of Lincoln and the fields around it. In the King's name they summoned the Earls and the greatest of the King's Reeves and Thanes; they summoned too, the leading churchmen; and they summoned the headmen of the largest towns. They summoned all the Great Men of England to the stone church, to give help and counsel to their King.

Like flames blown by the wind through the thatched roofs of a town, the news went faster than the messengers. Lincoln hummed with excitement and shuddered with dread. In every street armed men rode or tramped towards the top of the town; for the wooden steeple of Lincoln's stone church pointed to heaven from the top of Steep Hill.

Soon the churchyard and the marketplace were so crowded that it seemed that no one else could get in. But the King rode out of the castle with his guard of thirty thanes and three hundred spearmen; and his bodyguard forced a passage through the crowd with their spear-butts. King Godrich rode slowly across the marketplace to the door of the church; and he entered the church among his thanes.

In the church the Great Men of England knelt in humble greeting; but the King was grim; and he was dressed for war. Over his blue woollen tunic he wore a sleeveless leather byrnie with iron rings sewn on it; his long brown woollen stockings were cross-gartered from ankle to thigh with wide leather straps; and his red hair bushed out from beneath a pointed iron cap. A long sword with a gilded pommel hung ready at his side; and behind him his shield-bearer carried his round shield and long spear.

The King halted his horse in the middle of the nave and raised his hand for silence.

Then he spoke loudly, so that his harsh voice reached every man in the large church.

138

"Englishmen, once again the time has come when you must guard your lands and families against the pagan Danes. You all know how these heathen sea-robbers have raided our coast for two hundred years; you know how they have murdered holy men and stolen sacred treasure; you know how they have robbed churches and abbeys and burned farms and towns; you know how they have rounded up and slaughtered our sheep and cattle and carried off our women and children for slaves. Now the Vikings have come again, to break and burn, to slaughter and steal. I call upon you to follow me to Grimsby; for we must throw the devil's brood back into the sea, before they spread all over Lindsey. Come! Follow me! To horse and arms!" King Godrich cried.

Those warriors who liked the King's brave speech cheered loudly; and many waved their swords, crying: To horse and arms!' But the mightiest warrior of them all, Earl Leowulf, was sternly silent. He stood grimly in the doorway of the church, with a huge axe on his shoulder; and his Thanes and hearthmen stood watchfully around him. Leowulf raised his hand; the cheering faded to utter silence; and his deep voice boomed through the church:

"Lords and Masters, you all know me; and you know that I am ever at the front of any fight. None of you will dare to call me faint-hearted, if I ask you to wait a little while. So put up your swords; and hear my words."

"This is no time for words, men of England. This is a time for deeds, for bold deeds to save our homes and children from the black Danes," King Godrich shouted.

But Leowulf was loved by many there and respected by all; and the Earl of Essex said: "Let us hear Lord Leowulf! For he has always been the first to fight for us; and he has always counselled us well in war. But let his words be short!"

"Lords and Masters!" Leowulf said. "When we met in this town seven months ago, Earl Godrich of Cornwall told us a sad story. He told us that his ward, the Lady Goldenburg, although only a child, had defied him and had wedded a churl; and he told us that, for love of a pretty knave, she had given up her father's kingdom."

"Enough of this chatter!" King Godrich shouted. "We are here to fight the Danes, not to tell tales of girlish follies."

"Lords and warriors, Earl Godrich lied to us," Leowulf thundered. "That very day I spoke with the Lady Goldenburg; and she told me that her guardian had forced her to wed his kitchen-boy. My Masters,

140

how well the brave Earl's plan worked! For we never doubted his tearful tale; and we gave HIM the Lady's Kingdom. Godrich the Fox has made fools of us."

Leowulf paused to search the glum faces around him. Then he goaded them with words of scorn.

"I see that the truth is stale news to you, my Lords and Masters. Do you care so little that Earl Godrich has tricked the whole of England? Are you happy that he has shamed our Queen? Do you willingly serve a liar who is a traitor under our most sacred law?"

Leowulf paused again. Many of his hearers looked ashamed; but all avoided his stern eye; and King Godrich grinned triumphantly. Then, with a laugh which aroused even the sleepiest of his listeners, Leowulf went on.

"But did you know, Lords and Masters, that the cunning fox had overreached himself? Did you know that the 'churl' whom Godrich traitorously forced our Queen to wed was of King's blood? Did you know that that 'low-born knave' is the true-born King of all the Danes? Did you know that the Lady Goldenburg herself leads the Danish army which waits at Grimsby?"

There was a murmur of bewildered questioning among the crowd; and many smiled behind their hands at King Godrich's comical mistake. But no one dared to speak aloud against him.

"Lords and Masters, let us not fight against our rightful Queen!" Leowulf pleaded.

Then "Seize the traitor," Godrich shouted. But Leowulf was a fearsome sight, with his well-armed gang around him; and no one moved against him. Therefore Leowulf smiled and spoke on calmly:

"It is true that in years gone by we have suffered much from heathen robbers; but the Danes are now Christians as well as we. Let us not AGAIN play cat's paw for Earl Godrich! Let us not be tricked into defending his treachery with our life-blood! For the Danish army is here only to enforce Queen Goldenburg's undoubted right to England; and the Danish King has only one wish — to hang the thieving fox from the highest tree in Lincoln"

The faces turned towards Leowulf were friendly now; and Godrich chewed his beard in sullen silence. Therefore Leowulf felt sure of himself and gave the English firm advice.

"Let us send to Grimsby some worthy men who loved the good King Athelwald! Let our elders hear from the Lady Goldenburg herself how she was wedded and why she has brought a war-host to our shores! If the Lady wishes only to make good her rights against Earl Godrich, let a truce be made with the Danes! Then let the Lady Goldenburg find a champion, to uphold her claim in single combat against Earl Godrich! Let God be their judge!" Leowulf suggested.

"Seize the traitor," Godrich cried desperately. But the English leaders answered him: "Why should we fight and shed our life-blood, if war is unnecessary? We shall follow Earl Leowulf's counsel. If you shamed our Queen by wedding her to your kitchen-boy, you are a traitor; and you can fight for yourself; and may God be your judge! But, if Earl Leowulf has accused you falsely, then he must die a traitor's death."

"I am ready to die a shameful death, if I am wrong, Masters," Leowulf cried. "But see how Godrich scowls! The Fox is not so eager for the truth to be known. He does not want to defend his cause by himself; for he hoped to trick us into shielding him with our bodies. Let that lying fox be watched, Lords! Or he may slink away in the dark of night, dreading the dawn of truth."

To talk to Goldenburg the Great Men of England chose six men who had been her father's counsellors; and, because Thane Harald knew the countryside well, they asked him to guide the six old lords to Grimsby. Messengers were sent ahead to warn the

Danes that a peaceful band of English elders was coming to Grimsby; and Thane Harald led the elders across the Lincoln Wolds, guarded by his men.

As soon as Thane Harald reached Grimsby, he asked to be taken to the King of the Danes; for he wanted to arrange for the English elders to meet Goldenburg alone. But, when he was brought before the Danish King in Knut Grimson's hall, he hardly recognised his former kitchen-boy. For Olaf had become a man. His eyes were proud; his mouth was firm; and his chin now bore a bushy yellow beard. Furthermore, Olaf was richly dressed for war in the Danish style.

A short-sleeved mail shirt glinted like a silver net over a tight, sleeveless coat of black leather; and under his leather coat Olaf wore a long-sleeved tunic of thick red cloth. The mail covered his body only to the neck, the elbows and the knees. But a bib of leather, riveted with overlapping, crescent-shaped iron plates, guarded his throat and chest; heavy gold bracelets covered the red sleeves on his forearms; and leather shin-guards were tied tightly over his baggy trousers of bleached cloth.

Olaf's helmet was a domed cap of gilded iron plates riveted onto hoops of iron. The golden helmet fitted tightly on his brows and into the nape of his neck;

and it had a nose-piece which guarded his face. Across his knees there lay a broad axe, whose crescent-shaped blade was set on a haft of ash. A young man by his side carried his tall spear and handsome gilded shield.

Although Olaf was now a king, he got up from his seat and kissed Harald on both cheeks, saying cheerfully: "Welcome, noble Thane and foster-uncle!"

They talked of old times for a while; then Harald told Olaf his business. Olaf willingly gave leave for the English elders to talk to Goldenburg, sitting alone on the dais. But he remembered Leowulf's warning that Godrich might kill her; and he told the Grim sons to keep watch over her from the end of the hall. Then Olaf led Harald into the bower behind the dais. Olaf called for wine; but he spoke sternly to his old master.

"Why did these old men have to ride so far, to find out the truth about the Queen's wedding?" he asked the Thane. "For Godrich's chaplain, four of the Queen's women and you yourself were witnesses of that wedding; and you all heard how Godrich threatened to hang her if she refused."

For a moment Harald shifted his feet uneasily and stared at his hands. Then he looked Olaf straight in the eye. "I am Earl Godrich's man, King Olaf," he said firmly. "I and my father before me have done homage to him both for our thanedom and for our lands in Cornwall. Furthermore, it was Earl Godrich who, after King Athelwald died, made me Reeve of Lindsey. I cannot do anything against my own lord; and I shall fight faithfully at his side, so long as he is the rightful Earl of Cornwall. There are many in England who dislike the trick by which King Godrich ousted Queen Goldenburg. But the Earls and Headmen and all the Royal Thanes have sworn homage to Godrich as their King; and there are not many, I believe, who are willing to forswear their homage.

Few of us want to fight against Queen Goldenburg; for we all know that she is the rightful heir of King Athelwald. But fewer still would be willing to fight against King Godrich; for we are bound to him by oaths of service. Therefore, King Olaf, we hope that the quarrel between King Godrich and Queen Goldenburg will not bring war; and we hope that the quarrel can be settled in single combat between King Godrich and Queen Goldenburg's champion. God knows the truth. Let Him be the judge between them!"

"Amen to that!" said Olaf. Then he smiled and put his hand on Harald's shoulder. "I shall not ask you to break your oaths to Earl Godrich," he said. "But be as true to me, when I am King of England."

Olaf whispered to a page; and the page opened a chest by Olaf's bed. But Olaf himself turned back to Harald. "Last year, Thane Harald, when I was your servant, you gave me good woollen clothes and a silver brooch. Now I, still loving you although you serve my foe, give you this sable cloak and this gold brooch."

Harald took the rich cloak of dark brown fur and the heavy Irish brooch of enamelled gold; but he could not utter a word of thanks for this great gift and dumbly bowed his head, to hide his tears. Then suddenly, with a tender, moaning cry, he bent the knee and humbly placed Olaf's hand upon his head. Olaf's former master was ready to become his loyal man.

When Olaf and Harald returned to the hall, Goldenburg on her high seat was frowning angrily; and the six English elders standing at her feet were shaking their heads in woebegone dismay. "How Godrich fooled us!" they cried.

"But," said Goldenburg, "laughter follows sorrow. The sly fox fooled himself the more, when he forced me to wed his strongman kitchen boy; for neither Godrich nor I knew that that youth was born King of the Danes; and my husband has given me fifteen thousand trained warriors, to drag Godrich the Fox from his stolen seat."

"Fifteen thousand Vikings!" muttered the old lords, looking fearfully at one another; for the English war-host of farmers, artisans and noblemen's bodyguards could hardly hope to drive out such a veteran army. The English ambassadors hastily asked whether the Queen and her husband would agree to a truce; and they were happy to see that Queen Goldenburg still smiled at them.

"We will make a truce gladly, Lords," she said. "We have no wish to lay waste with war our own Kingdom of England. Indeed, everything needed by the Danish war-host has already been paid for with my husband's gold."

The English elders were dumbfounded. They had never heard of an army which paid for what it needed; for usually war-hosts not only stole whatever they wanted but broke and burned everything else. The elders thought that Olaf might be a good king, even though he was a Dane. Therefore they bowed respectfully to Olaf and invited him to speak.

"But THIS is your Queen," said Olaf, pointing. "Hear what SHE has to say."

"As your rightful Queen," Goldenburg said sternly: "I say that Godrich, Earl of Cornwall, is a false traitor and an oath-breaker. If anyone in England doubts that indictment, my champion, King Olaf himself, will prove my words upon Godrich's body. Set out the hazel sticks on some grassy hill near Lincoln and Grimsby; and there, in the sight of both the English and the Danish lords, let God show the right!"

When the six old lords went back to Lincoln, they told the Witenagemot Queen Goldenburg's words. The English leaders did not want their lands wasted and their men killed in a useless war; and they told King Godrich that they would not fight on his behalf, unless he first defeated the Queen's champion. Proudly King Godrich threw back his head.

"Do you think that I, the winner of 100 fights, am afraid to meet this sparsely bearded kitchen-boy? Last year he was turning a spit in my kitchen; but tomorrow I shall spit HIM on my spear," he boasted.

Each side chose a marshal, to arrange and control the trial by battle; and the marshals told Thane Harald to find a battlefield.

He chose a flat hilltop, where the grass had been cropped short by sheep; and he marked out the bounds of the field of combat with peeled hazel rods stuck into the ground. On the day of the trial the leaders of both hosts rode out from Lincoln and Grimsby onto the Wolds. They left their weapons and their horses with their spearmen at the foot of the hill; and they gathered unarmed and on foot around the hazelled field.

At midday the two Kings with their shield-bearers rode up and dismounted at opposite ends of the field. The Archbishop of York, in a litter shouldered by four black-robed monks, was carried onto the field; and the two marshals rode out with a herald.

First, the herald sounded his trumpet for silence.

"Kings, Lords and Masters!" he cried and read out in a high singsong voice the terms of the truce agreed between the two sides. Then all present raised their right hands and swore to keep peace at the hazelled field; and they swore to go home peacefully, whatever the outcome of the trial.

Again the herald sounded his trumpet; and the two Kings took their shields and their long spears from their pages. Then the Archbishop called upon Almighty God to watch the trial and to show clearly which side was right; and he blessed both the combatants and the whole gathering, before he left the field. Lastly the marshals rode to the boundary stakes and blew a long blast on their hunting horns.

At that signal the two Kings ran eagerly towards the middle of the field. A sheathed sword hung at Godrich's side; and a broad axe hung at Olaf's; but both Kings held ten-foot spears in their right hands and leather-covered limewood shields in their left hands. The round shields they held before their faces; but the long spears were drawn back behind their shoulders, to give more power to their thrusts.

For an hour the champions hurled and lunged fiercely with their spears and parried and blocked with their shields; and they gave each other many small flesh wounds but no crippling injuries. By then their beards dripped sweat; and their throats were dry with their panting breath. Though still strong, they were very weary.

At last Godrich broke off the fight and walked ten paces away from Olaf, to regain his breath. He stuck his spear into the turf and lowered his shield, in order to rest his arms at his sides. For a while Olaf watched him. Then suddenly he gathered his strength and flung his heavy spear like a thunderbolt.

The spear struck Godrich a sidelong blow on the neck and opened a bloody gash below his ear.

Godrich stumbled; but he kept his feet; and, before Olaf could unhook his axe from his belt, Godrich ran at him and speared him through the thigh. Godrich twisted his spear and, shouting triumphantly, hurled Olaf sprawling on the ground. Although Olaf tried to guard himself with his shield, Godrich speared him again and again.

Olaf's battle-shirt of iron mail had been made by a master craftsman in the Rhinelands; and, although he was gashed about the legs, he was not disabled. Suddenly he threw away his shield, in order to grasp Godrich's spear-shaft with his left hand. With a jerk and a spring he pulled himself up onto his feet. Then with his axe he struck the blade from Godrich's spear.

Now it was Godrich whose right hand held no weapon; and, as he felt for his sword, he crouched low under cover of his shield. Olaf stepped in close and swung his axe with both hands. The axe struck Godrich on his shoulders and knocked him to his knees; but his tough leather-and-iron byrnie turned the axe's edge; and the blow only bruised him.

Dizzily Godrich pushed himself to his feet, with his shield held above his head. But, even as he rose, Olaf's axe split his shield to the iron boss which guarded his hand. Nevertheless, Godrich stepped back unharmed; and his right hand had found his sword-hilt.

When Godrich had drawn his sword, it rang against Olaf's axe in well-matched strife.

For Godrich, wielding both sword and shield, could guard himself against Olaf's double-handed axe; and Olaf's young legs kept him safe from Godrich's slashing sword. But Olaf was shieldless; and Godrich's shield was held together only by the central iron handle and its guardian boss. The watching warriors asked one another which would fail first— Olaf's youthful speed or Godrich's riven shield.

For a second hour the two Kings fought, until the grass sparkled with sheared iron rings and glistened with blood. Godrich's head hung low; and his sword-arm was weary and slow to strike. But Olaf's legs too were trembling tired, as he danced dizzily around his enemy. Time after time Olaf had darted in, to strike a blow, and was away before Godrich's sword could catch him. But Godrich was content to defend himself. He was saving his strength for the time when Olaf's legs grew weak; for then Olaf, without a shield, would be at his mercy.

Olaf also knew that time was not his friend. "Father, help me," he whispered urgently. Then, gritting his teeth, he sprang upon Godrich. He swung his axe at Godrich's head; and Godrich parried it with his sword as well as with his faulty shield. But this time Olaf did not dodge away. Although Godrich's sword struck into his ribs, he swung his axe again and again and yet again; and at last his blade found the gaping split in Godrich's shield and sliced it clean in two. Through iron, sinew and bone the axe-blade sheared; and Godrich's cloven shield, with his severed hand still gripping the handle, fell to the ground.

Again Olaf swung his axe; and Godrich raised his sword, to guard his head. But the axe ran down the sword-blade and sheared the fingers of Godrich's right hand on the hilt. Godrich's sword — and four fingers too — fell onto the grass.

All in a moment Godrich was maimed and defenceless. The watching Englishmen told one another that the gods had taken an awful revenge on him for disparaging the queen. For now Godrich was altogether helpless before his enemy; and his strong body could be made to suffer much pain and shame, before he died. But Olaf felt no need to prolong his vengeance; and he shouted clearly, so that all on the field could hear his offer: "Yield, Godrich, Earl of Cornwall; and the Earls of England shall deem your doom for your crime against the Queen."

Godrich had always lived close to pain and death; and he feared neither. He blew his red whiskers from his mouth and growled: "No man shall ever say that Godrich, King of England, yielded to his kitchen-boy. Give me a quick death, strongman; and bury me in consecrated ground."

Calmly Godrich turned aside and bowed his head; and neatly Olaf struck it from his shoulders. At the moment of King Godrich's death a long-drawn moan arose from the Englishmen around the field; for all had sworn him homage. "Ahhh!" they sighed. Then, "The Fair Goldenburg is our Queen; and Strongman Olaf is our King," they cried. And the Danes shouted triumphantly: "Olaf the Strong! Olaf the Strong! Olaf the Strong! King of all the Danes and all the English too!"

Goldenburg gathered in her hands the long skirts of her gown and kirtles. Awkwardly she ran across the field; and the crowd rejoiced to see that their queen was great with child. Then Leowulf took her arm, to help her. "Strongman Olaf is my Lord!" Leowulf roared; and he waved his hood around his head.

Olaf King-born, with his chest heaving and with the dark blood clotting on his clothes, stood leaning on his axe. His head was bowed thoughtfully; for he was gazing at the dead man lying at his feet. Olaf felt no joy at having killed Godrich. He felt only a great peace. For he had at last fulfilled the kingly fate to which he had been born; and the ancient gods, his forefathers, no longer drove him on.

However, when Olaf saw his wife running towards him, he threw down his axe and pushed the helmet from his head. Then with wide-flung arms he gathered her to his bloody chest and laughed for pure delight.

THE END

ABOUT THE AUTHOR

Ian Fraser was born into a well-known Scottish family, of which practically every man for more than seven hundred years had been a warrior. But, because his father was disinherited for choosing the 'cowardly' profession of clergyman, the author was brought up and educated in southern England. During the war he was an officer in the Royal Navy (actually a 'torpedo pilot' in the Fleet Air Arm) and in 1943 both decorated with the Distinguished Service Cross and captured. After two + years as a German P.O. W., he became an administrator in the British Colonial Service, working primarily in Malaysia and Singapore. There, he met and worked amongst simple people comparable to our ancestors of a thousand years ago. He was deeply impressed by how vastly different human beings are in different times and places and by the utter fallacy of the assumption that all men are, and always have been, the same. He was honoured as an Officer of the Order of the British Empire in 1960 and later served in Aden and the Bahamas.

The Stranger Warrior

This is an exciting historical tale for older children based on a famous British legend, with the background of life in the British Isles in about 900A.D. as full and accurate as present knowledge allows.

The hero, Horn, is orphaned and cast adrift when a Viking fleet conquers the Isle of Man for the King of Norway. Because Horn has neither land nor treasure, he pursues his sacred duty of revenge by striving to become a famous warrior. He serves both an English elderman and an Irish king, rejecting comfort and love in his search for fame; at last after many battles he avenges his father, reconquers the Isle of Man and – almost incidentally – collects a bride.

Tristan the Lover

The minstrels' story of Tristan and Isolt was written down in French and German in the 11th century. It was later incorporated, with many other stories, into 'The Arthurian legend' – the adventures of King Arthur's Knights of the Round Table.

Mallory's 'Morte d'Arthur' was one of the first books in English which was printed instead of copied by hand. Mallory's book both popularised the Arthurian legend and buried the 11th century manuscripts of the Tristan tale.

"Tristan the Lover", retells the 11th century version.